INNER SPACES

INNER SPACES

New Writing by Women from Kerala

Editorial Board
K. M. GEORGE
JANCY JAMES
VASANTHI SANKARANARAYANAN
RAJ KAMINI MAHADEVAN

kali for women

1993

*Inner Spaces : New Writing
by Women from Kerala* **was
first published in 1993 by**

**Kali for Women
A 36 Gulmohar Park
New Delhi 110049**

ISBN 81-85107-43-2

Typeset by Futura Graphics
D-40, Greater Kailash, Enclave-II, New Delhi-110 048 and
Printed at Crescent Printing Works (P) Ltd
New Delhi 110 001

Contents

FOREWORD

Kerala is a narrow strip of land on the south-west coast of India, lying between the Western Ghats and the Arabian Sea. In an area of nearly 39,00,000 square kilometres, live 2.91 crore people. Kerala has been among the most vibrant and problematic states in the Indian Union since Independence, and perhaps one reason for this is the combination of high literacy and low per capita income, making the people conscious of their claims for a minimum standard of life. On the face of it, Kerala appears to be a place of paradoxes: the land is fertile, but the people are poor, the percentage of literacy is the highest in India (now 100 per cent), but one comes across the most orthodox and superstitious people along with the most modern and revolutionary kind. The land is very beautiful and so are its people. Its lovely lagoons and backwaters, and its colourful landscape continue to charm tourists. Kerala, very much a part of India, nonetheless has its own distinctive sub-culture with its special customs and manners. In short, it is a veritable museum of seeming incongruities providing a rich field of research for the sociologist.

What, then, is the social position of women in this state and what their literary contribution? Are these different from the rest of India and if so, why and how? These are not easy questions, but an attempt to answer them or at least to understand them in the Indian context is not only a worthwhile proposition but an intriguing one.

Kerala's geographical position has, to some extent, provided circumstances conducive to a kind of cultural isolation because it has been shielded by the Western Ghats. There have, however, also been contacts with the outside world by means of the Arabian Sea. Several peoples and races have contributed to make Kerala's culture composite and cosmopolitan. As compared to the rest of India, Kerala represents a different complexion in the disposition of major communities. Muslims form 10 per cent of the population in India and Christians a bare 2.5, the vast majority being Hindus. In Kerala however, Christians can claim a population of 21 per cent and Muslims 19 per cent. Scheduled Castes and Tribes together constitute about 10 per cent. The Hindus are divided into a number of castes and sub-castes and the caste distinctions have reached such a deplorable level that Swami Vivekananda was forced to remark even towards the end of the last century that Kerala was a lunatic asylum!

Another significant aspect of culture is the joint family (matrilocal) setup, and the matrilineal system of inheritance followed by the major community of Nairs and partially also by certain other castes such as the Ezhavas. We need not go into the many theories of the origins of this sytem; suffice it to say that the women were the custodians of the family property and even the *karanavar*, who was the seniormost male member of the joint family, was only a manager who helped the custodian in the administration of income and expenditure. 'In polyandry, as in promiscuity, maternity alone is an undisputed fact, and paternity becomes at best a matter of conjecture.' Whatever the historical background, women in Kerala, at least in some of the major communities, can be said to have shared more power than their counterparts in the rest of India.

Malayalam, the mother tongue of 96 per cent of the people of Kerala, is a highly Sanskritised member of the Dravidian family. It is considerably indebted to Sanskrit not only for its rich vocabulary but also for its literary forms, especially of the medieval period. The modern period commences with the impact of Western culture, which was brought to bear on Malayalam literature with the spread of Western education in the early decades of the nineteenth century. It was the European missionaries of Protestant fold who took the initiative in this regard. Thus, Kerala stands in the forefront of Indian states in the matter of literacy and education.

It is interesting to see how literacy is shared between men and women in Kerala in comparison with certain other states and the country as a whole.*

In the years after Independence, there has been visible progress in literacy for women, even though they rank lower everywhere. Taking only the 1981 position, we see that the literacy level for women in India is about half that of men (24.8 and 46.9) whereas in Kerala it is 88 per cent of the rate for men (65.7 and 75.3). In other words, women in Kerala have a much better position where literacy is concerned, in comparison with their counterparts in other states. Starting with their 60 per cent to that of men in 1951 they reached 88 per cent in 1981. This progress is also reflected in jobs held by women and hopefully the day is not far off when they will equal men in professional occupations and attainments.

Do we find a similar, parallel progress in women writing in Kerala? We will come back to this question.

Male domination is conspicuous in every branch of every literature. This we see not only in the production of literary works, but even in the approach to literature, literary theories and perceptions. Curiously enough, certain aspects of grammar, idiomatic expression and symbols are so male-oriented that women find it difficult to use them appropriately. This gender-specific colour is common to all languages.

* Growth of literacy

Years	Kerala			Karnataka			Tamilnadu			India		
	P	M	F	P	M	F	P	M	F	P	M	F
1951	40.7	50.2	31.5	19.3	29.1	9.2	20.8	31.6	10.0	16.6	24.9	7.9
1961	46.8	55.0	38.9	29.8	42.3	16.7	36.4	51.6	21.1	24.0	34.5	13.0
1971	60.4	66.6	54.3	31.5	41.6	21.0	39.5	51.8	26.9	29.5	39.5	18.7
1981	70.4	75.3	65.7	38.5	48.8	27.7	46.8	58.3	35.0	36.1	36.1	24.8

P-Person,   M-Males,   F-Female

(Statistics taken from *Women in Kerala*-1989 Department of Economics and Statistics, Trivandrum 1989).

However, there have been some significant literary efforts by women in the nineteenth and twentieth centuries. They fall into two categories, discursive and creative. Both these categories received a fillip with the emergence of periodicals specifically addressed to women.

The main purpose of the early women's periodicals in India was to champion women's education, to condemn social practices and customs that were discriminatory and to encourage self-expression. Some of the important magazines that came up in the different languages are: *Satihitabodhini* (Telugu, 1883), *Bharati* (Bengali, 1884), *Keraliya Sugunabodhini* (Malayalam, 1887), *Penmatibodhini* (Tamil, 1891), *Indian Ladies Magazine* (English, 1901), *Sarada* (Malayalam, 1904), *Stridarpan* (Hindi, 1909), *Karnataka Nandini* (Kannada, 1917).

In addition to the above, several other periodicals came up in most of these languages, while a few of them closed down after some years. In some cases the periodicals were edited by men (as in the case of *Sugunabodhini*) though they catered to the interests of women. All the major languages of India were brought into the service of this cause either towards the end of the last century or the beginning of this one. As well, in some general magazines, space was reserved for women's writing.

Women writing in Malayalam

In addition to *Sugunabodhini* and *Sarada* there are also other periodicals in Malayalam which served women for some years. Some of these, which were edited and controlled by women included: (*Lakshmibai*, 1905), (*Mahilaratnam*, 1916), (*Mahila*, 1921), (*Sahodari*, 1925), (*Mahilamandiram*, 1927), (*Malayala Manika*, 1931), (*Stri*, 1933).

Informative articles on literacy and education for women, health, child-rearing and other similar subjects were published in these periodicals as well as in those edited by men. They mainly covered the area of discursive writings. It was only later, around the 1930s, a period that is seen as part of the early phase of the women's movement, that women started publishing stories and poems through some of these periodicals. Thereafter, a change was noticed, as women's perspectives began to enter the field of writing.

There have been examples of creative expression by women in the composition of songs and poems as also in some plays. But these received scant encouragement from established male writers. As Lalithambika Antharjanam, one of the best known writers in Kerala, observed, 'In the literary world, women writers were considered in the category of scheduled castes and tribes.'

This attitude changed when Lalithambika and a few others started writing short stories in the thirties and forties. In the last fifty to sixty years, women writing in Malayalam, particularly fiction writers, have assumed a significant position, and it is important to assess their position in the overall context.

The short story in Malayalam is quite a developed branch of literature. The impact of the West is clearly visible in the blossoming of the modern short story. Its history of about a hundred years can perhaps be considered in four phases: the early pioneers were Kesari Nayanar, Oduvil Kunjukrishna Menon, M.R.K.C., Ampadi Narayana Poduval, K. Sukumaran and E.V. Krishna Pillai. They modelled themselves on Hawthorne, Edgar Allan Poe and other such writers, and their main aim was to provide entertainment. The second phase begins with the thirties when writers with progressive ideas such as Thakazhi, Kesava Dev, Ponkunnam Varki, Basheer, S.K. Pottekkad, Karoor and others came on the scene. They wrote on realistic themes of local interest and emphasised characterisation. Gorky, Chekhov and Maupassant were their models. The third phase is a natural continuation of the second. Here, the story writers are not necessarily wedded to a commitment to socialist realism. Writers like M.T. Vasudevan Nair, T. Padmanabhan, K. Surendran, and N.P. Muhammed, come under this category. Their heyday was in the fifties and sixties. From the seventies on there are experimentalists like George Kakkanadan, Anand,

Mukundan and Zachariah who are inspired, among other things, by surrealism, naturalism, existentialism and other creative processes as they probe the intricacies of human behaviour.

Under each category, other than the first, even the names of outstanding writers would exceed a score. The names of women writers have not figured in the list. There is no one in the first phase. In the second phase, the names of Lalithambika Antharjanam and K. Saraswati Amma could be mentioned. And in subsequent phases, several women writers deserve places of importance. In quality they equal male writers, though in quantity their total output is probably not even a tenth of the output of men.

Both male and female writers however, write on similar subjects: men and women, their inter-relations in circumstances which would interest human beings of all categories. But, generally speaking, man's eye is different to that of the woman's although, of course, both are capable of looking at things from each other's points of view. Perhaps it is the lens that is different.

Men writers have occasionally shown the rare gift of seeing social circumstances through a woman's eyes. Let me cite one example from Malayalam fiction.

Indulekha, (1889) by Chandu Menon is the most significant early novel in Malayalam. (English translation: Mathrubhumi Publishers, Calicut). Though Menon followed the pattern of the English novel, he selected a local theme so that his readers would be directly interested. His examination of the social and cultural life around him led him to conclude that things had degenerated considerably in the social structure of the two predominant communities of Nairs and Nambudiris. Nair women (belonging to respectable families) were treated merely as playthings by high caste Nambudiris and Nair parents considered this too venerable a tradition to be broken. The Nambudiris, who entered into a special marriage relationship called '*sambandham*', had no responsibility as husbands except to beget children. And the women had no choice. The matrilineal system helped this lopsided arrangement. The novel *Indulekha* came as a literary bomb in the *sambandham* fortress.

Another very significant aspect of the novel is the creation of the character Indulekha. Mature, brilliant, well bred and erudite, Indulekha makes a fool of her Nambudiri suitor with a repartee and wit which is scintillating and she also has the courage to refuse the patriarchal dictates of her grand uncle, Panchu Menon.

Even her lover Madhavan, who is the nominal hero, is not equal to her in sagacity or self-assurance. So she has the last word in the choice of her life-partner.

In the last hundred years many men and women have created women characters of high quality in Malayalam fiction. But no character equals Indulekha in dignity, composure and independence. Chandu Menon had no idea of feminism. But his contribution to the thought process is important.

Our women writers too have created women characters who have challenged men and circumstances. But so far, it has been difficult to rival the character of Indulekha. It is in this context that we have to examine the fifteen stories by women writers that have been selected for the present Anthology.

* * * *

We have already referred to the two areas of women's writing in Malayalam, namely, the discursive and creative. Most of the material published in the women's magazines of the late nineteenth and early twentieth centuries, was of the informative and discursive kind. Creative writing by women had a regular flow only from the thirties on. The discursive variety of writing (of the early period) has been practically forgotten. However, a good percentage of stories and poems produced from the thirties are still remembered, re-published and read. There are also a few novels and plays written by women which are quite popular, but the richest genre of literature by women in Kerala is undoubtedly the short-story. From an existing repertoire of about 2000 short stories written by women in the last six decades, it has not been easy for the editors to select fifteen for this anthology. What is included here, although not comprehensive, provides a good range: from the veteran Lalithambika Antharjanam who started writing stories in the thirties to the modernist Sara Joseph, there is sufficient variety to reflect the composite complexion of women's stories in Malayalam.

Lalithambika Antharjanam's story *The Admission of Guilt* with which this collection opens, is a moving account of a Nambudiri widow, who is questioned by the powerful village council for suspected adultery. Although not a rebel, the protagonist is aware of her rights as a human being and refuses to name her partner, preferring instead to cherish the few moments of love he has given her. This story is, in some ways, typical of Lalithambika's works which are known for their sympathetic portrayal of women in the Nambudiri community and their oppression by a crumbling but powerful tradition. In *When Dreams Turn Live* Sara Thomas gives expression to the feelings of an old, lonely widow who prepares to welcome her children and grandchildren home for their annual visit at Onam, and is deeply hurt by the revelation of their 'indifference'. In Shobha Warrier's simple but realistically designed short story *Granny* we meet the proverbial destitute Brahmin widow, who symbolises many like her who are forced to toil for mere survival. *Granny* is followed by B. Saraswathy's *The Fisherman* in which Kalyani, a young woman, lives a life of endless toil for her good-for-nothing drunkard-husband, cherishing the precious few moments of the man's devotion and concern for her.

Here are four very different women: the Nambudiri widow who suffers because of a lopsided tradition, the ageing mother whose world centres around her increasingly distant children, the near-blind grandmother forced to work for a living, the fisherwoman who tolerates a crude and unsympathetic husband. None of them is openly protesting or defiant, yet each manages to communicate to the reader the core of strength that lies at the heart of her being.

The next 'group' of stories marks a more open and stronger voice of protest, whether it is against the protagonist's personal circumstances or against society. K. Saraswathi Amma is known as the first feminist satirist of Malayalam literature. Her story, *The Soil that Grows Diamonds* is a powerful critique of our society in which a poor woman is forced to barter her body for survival. The poignancy of the story lies in the woman's own acceptance of this: as all those who claim to be dear to her cash in on her body, she confronts their hypocrisy by scornfully claiming her body to be 'the soil that grows diamonds'. Bold, outspoken, unconventional and fiercely independent, K. Saraswathi Amma defied the conventions of a normal aristocratic upbringing, and expressed her disapproval of male dominance without reserve.

In *The Stone Woman* K.B. Sreedevi has chosen to hit out at the false morality imposed on women by husbands who wield power and prestige. In her story, Ahalya, a mythical character, unfairly cursed to turn into stone because of her supposedly 'unchaste' behaviour (she became involved with the god Indra who came to her in the form of her husband), chooses to remain a stone woman in solidarity with Sita, (also a mythical character) whose chastity is held suspect by her husband, the god Ram, who is the only one who has the power to bring Ahalya back to life. Rather, than be indebted to one who has been unfair to his own wife, Ahalya remains a stone woman.

M.D. Retnamma's *The Cow* bristles with sarcasm: a caricature of the groom develops as the author shows the increasing anger and despair of the new bride at being ignored. The next story in this group, *In the Temple* by Rajalekshmy, subtly exposes the hypocrisy and empty ritualism of religion, as well as the worthlessness of an indifferent god. *Incomplete Stops* by Ashita tells the story of a woman who is summarily released from a mental hospital where she found herself after being abandoned by her husband, and points an uncompromising finger at society and all those who are complicit in devaluing this woman's life and desires.

The next few stories can be said to represent a kind of exploration of the self, a search for truth. Realism and fantasy are interwoven here, and linear time often ceases to have meaning, with the imagination sometimes moving back and forth between life and death, past and future. . .

Kamala Das who is widely known as a poet and writer in English, writes in Malayalam under the name, Madhavi Kutty. In *The Game of Chess* she looks at how, while extra-marital love defies societal bounds, it is both liberating and constraining for women. *Chamundi's Pit* by Vatsala seems at one level, to be simply the experience of an illiterate woman trying to escape the hardship and drudgery of her life. But the story is also a search for self and the realisation of inner and outer spaces is suggested through the symbolism of water — which becomes central to the life giving function. The cool, life sustaining water then becomes the thread connecting man to woman.

P.R. Shyamala's story *The Guest who Came in a Palanquin* has a special dimension. It reads like an old tale where an aristocratic, benevolent lady promises to redeem her young maid who has 'gone astray'. Here the author plays with the time sequence, using deliberate generalisation and omission, and thus maintains an ambiguity which allows many conclusions and in fact becomes a ploy whereby the victim becomes the victor and the vanquished the van-quisher. In the next story, *The Third Night* Nalini Bakel uses the journey as a symbol of life's exploration. The protagonist's long bus journey becomes a metaphorical excursion and dream of reunion with her lover, which terminates in a nowhere land.

The Sword of the Princess by Manasi is a many-layered story which interweaves dreams with fantasy and reality with dreams. The last story in this collection, Sarah Joseph's *The Symphony of the Forest* speaks of the conflict and dilemmas of the woman who is torn between home and family and her yearning for something more meaningful, less routine.

As we have seen, these stories do not fall neatly into any particular category, because there is always overlap of one kind or another. Nalini Bakel's story *The Third Night* and Rajalekshmy's *In the Temple* are really love stories. Indeed, whether it is the quiet pain of love or open protest and challenge against a social system, or even the abstract and indirect expression of life's complexities through fantasy and symbol, the stories present a point of view that is unique to women. Not only are all the protagonists female, but by and large, their search for meaning in their lives, or for liberation does not take the shape of imitating the male idea of freedom and power. It is also important to note that the writers do not at any point, become mere message bearers of feminism. They are, primarily, creative writers.

Taken together, the stories here reflect the range and sophistication which has become characteristic of women short story writers in Malayalam. Of course translations inevitably mean a loss of flavour and nuance, that so enriches the original, but the editors have attempted here to maintain, as far as possible, the temper and texture of creative writing by women in Kerala.

K.M.George

The Admission of Guilt

LALITHAMBIKA ANTARJANAM

The object, detained and tried by the people's court, for suspected adultery, made the following statement:

'I am guilty. You can expel me from the caste. The fault is entirely mine. No one else is a party to this crime.'

The assembly of Brahmin priests was shocked. What arrogance! A pregnant widow claiming that no one else was partner in her guilt. In that case, was she guilty at all?

The prosecutor of the *Smartha* trial roared, 'Adultress! You have gone astray. At least now, tell us the truth.'

From the inner precincts of the fifth house a hesitant voice emerged:

'God is my witness, when I say that I do not know who the offenders are in this case. The loneliness of that night? My youth? The forceful urge of some emotion, not known or experienced? You all know that I am a child widow. My *tali* was removed when I was barely fourteen. Twenty years have passed since then. In that time, have I done anything to bring a bad name to myself? I have meticulously observed the fasts of Monday and *Pradosham*. The *Magha* bathing and the *Vaisakha* penance have been regular rituals. Have I ever failed to perform the Monday worship at Triprangode and Guruvayoor? Why, then, did the Lord impel me to act as I did, just for that one night? I haven't talked to any man, other than my father. I was afraid even to think about men. There is only one man a woman ought to know. And I did not have that man.

'My world was confined to the kitchen and the *Vadakkini*. Never have I dared to open the door of the *Nalukettu* and look out at the world. Why did this happen to me? I will tell you that story. Whether you believe it or not, it is the truth.'

An unusual defense. The court was stunned. How can this fallen Namboodiri woman justify such a clear indisputable accusation of misconduct?

The priest gave his consent in an irritated tone, 'Say whatever you have to say, and do it soon.'

The door to the women's quarters opened a little. Through the wedge, words gushed forth into the outer world like a river in spate.

'I am aware that you think that listening to my story, why, even hearing my words, is a sin. At one time, I too believed that an ostracised Namboodiri woman is more despicable and contemptible than the evil spirits themselves. I myself took care not to be contaminated by stories of such women or even by the wind which blew from that direction. I never visited Tatri Edathi even when she was on her deathbed. Perhaps it is that great sin, which I am paying for now . . . .

'I will not relate that story now. You were all present for Atiri's *Vavam*. On that day, why was such a marriage fixed? It was an exchange of women—the thirty-year old daughter of the elder Namboodiri to my house and me, eleven years and three months old, to the old man of that house. An exchange devised so that the fathers of both the houses could get married once again. My grandmother used to say, "We were lucky that at least Kutty married before she reached puberty. But I am worried about how she will live with those uncaring people."

'I did not have to live there long. My father's new wife—my second mother—or rather my husband's daughter, was a sickly woman. She died soon. I became a burden to the elder

Namboodiri. In such a situation, women usually go back to their parent's home. Since my mother still happened to be my father's favourite wife, my happiness was assured.

'I have seen my husband's face only once. I was more perplexed than afraid when I saw his white beard, his moustache and the pot belly. I did not step into the room he slept in, even though my grandmother tried to persuade me to do so several times. After that day, he, who had four legitimate and forty casual relationships never came to my house. Perhaps it was because of that curse, that after two years . . .

'A messenger came to our house, during the Onam festival while I was playing with a ball in the courtyard. I saw father whispering something into mother's ears. "Oh! my child! What a betrayal! My Lord Siva!" Mother swooned, beating her breasts. People thronged around her. Everyone seemed to be whispering. I continued to play with my friends, uncaring. Someone dragged me inside. A loud chorus of wailing arose from the kitchen. I did not cry. Why should I have done?

'I bathed, and while still in my wet clothes, was led down into a dark room. I removed my bronze bracelets and wiped the vermilion mark from my forehead. I did whatever they asked me to do. But when the mistress of rituals was about to cut the black thread worn round the neck, I protested. "I will not give this. I can't give my *tali*. Ask my mother. This is the thread I hold on to, when I say my evening prayers."

'Even my father was informed of my stubbornness. He came and stood at the door, his face lined with the tiredness of old age and coaxed me, "Give it child. Let them take away that useless thread. I will buy you a new chain—a better one—after ten days."

'I knew that my father would keep his promise. After the rituals were over a *tulasi* chain in gold was given to me, to replace that broken *tali*. That chain glittered and shone. How easy it was to satisfy my desire for adornment! Even today, how I wish I had not found out the difference between that *tali* and this chain.

'Soon, I learnt of the changes I had to make in my lifestyle.

I was not to touch the eight auspicious objects or the lamp. Wearing kohl and kumkum were forbidden. A full meal could be eaten only once a day. Thus, my grandmother taught me all that was expected of me, in dress, behaviour and demeanour. Often, I would lie on her lap, listening to old stories. I heard, for the first time, stories of Krishna, the Gopikas and their Vrindavanam. Grandmother always wound up the story wistfully, saying "Chant the name of the Lord, Krishna, Guruvayoorappa. That is your fate."

'I asked, "Where is the God, grandmother?"

"Everywhere. If you pray hard enough, you too can see Him."

"Can I?" I would listen carefully. "Have you seen Him, grandmother?"

"Me? Am I that lucky, child? But people like Bhattatirippad have said while reading the epics, that they have seen him. His yellow silk dress, the peacock feather and the divine flute! Sri Krishna! Hari Krishna! Krishna! Krishna!"

'Grandmother would then close her eyes in reverence and clasp her prayer beads with trembling fingers. At such times I felt that she actually saw the Lord standing before her. I am not familiar with the stories related by Bhattatirippad. Still, I felt this attraction for Sri Krishna. Is there a young girl who is not attracted to this young cowherd, who sang and danced?

'In my house, I am in charge of the puja. Early in the morning, after a bath, I made the garlands, lit the lamps, and anointed the images of the Gods. Out of the innumerable idols, my favourite one was that of Vishnu with Lakshmi, the god of Love smiling at and embracing the goddess with the same hands that held the conch and the wheel! I was aroused by that sight. Every day, I placed a garland on that shining idol and put a saffron mark on its forehead. Thus, in that prayer room all my suppressed desires for adornment were revived and became acts of devotion. In those dreamy mornings and evenings, filled with the fragrance of the flowers of worship and the warm glow of the lamps and the incense, as I leaned in front of the beautiful idol, I was seized by a vague desire. Why can't I wear in my hair, the garlands used for worship the day before? Or wear a castemark of sandalwood paste? No, that was not possible. I could have only the ashes of burnt desires.

'Even when she was on her death-bed, my grandmother was concerned about me. "Son, please take special care of her. She is young."

'No one thought then, how prophetic those words would turn out to be; like words uttered by fate itself. Only I had a premonition of disaster. Why should they have to take special care of me? I, who was so modest and guileless.

'The years passed uneventfully and I was not aware that the child in me had become a young woman. Days rolled on and saw me immersed in bathing, worship and prayer. It never occurred to me to pay attention to myself till my brother married and brought his bride home. Why was my sister-in-law so beautiful? Why did she laugh so gaily? Every evening she had a wash and decorated her hair with jasmine garlands. Her gold bordered cloth was pleated and worn gracefully. A new way of life, unknown to me, unfolded in front of my eyes. Every night, when the doors of their room banged shut, the sound reverberated in my ears ... please do not be angry with me. I am saying this out of sorrow. I am not jealous of my sister-in-law or anyone else. Still, when I think of the difference in what life offered to us, my inner being breaks down. After all there is an age difference of only six months between us.

'A widow is more scared of laughter than of tears. Merry-making by anyone—whoever it is—pains her. To stand aside and watch someone else—however dear that person may be—enjoy the pleasures and happiness denied to oneself forever... blessed priests, do you know how gross is the pain and agony of such an experience? It is this fire of agony that burns inside the women's quarters of Namboodiri houses. The reasons were many. I couldn't get, from my favourite creeper, even a single jasmine blossom for worship. The first bloom of the champaka tree, which I had painstakingly nurtured, was missing. My agony and irritation became unbearable and I grumbled.

"Which beauty is stealing my flowers meant for worship and dolling herself up? This is not what I grew these flowers for."

"Why grow jasmine if it cannot be worn by newly weds? Just because you are not allowed to deck yourself up, you should not grumble like this."

'A piercing reply which sowed the seeds of internal discord in the house. My sister-in-law and I used to fight over trivial things; our fights ended in tears or curses for each other. Invariably, I won. That was natural as my mother and father were then alive. My sister-in-law, thus outwitted, would bite her teeth and murmur.

"All right. One day I'll get even. You wait and see."

'Yes, I have been a victim of the cruelty of those well designed revenges. Probably I have had more than my share. All you Namboodiris know the place given to women in their natal homes. The ill treatment meted out in one's own *tarawad* forces most of us to go and live in our husband's houses. As long as our parents are alive, we do not suffer in our own homes. We even succeed in outwitting the brides who are brought into the house. But when the father's younger brother takes charge of the house, everything changes.

'Everyone then tries to flatter his wife and children to make things easy for themselves. The son of the house has the final say. We become the helpless victims of kitchen quarrels and run hither and thither for shelter. Even a housemaid can concoct lies and admonish widows. I saw all this and experienced all kinds of suffering. In the year after my mother's death, I left the house in tears.

'My husband's brood of daughters, six or seven girls from his three marriages had all come of age. Four co-sisters, wives, eight or ten children—four daughters older than I—I also joined them. From every corner of that house, dilapidated through rain and neglect, one could only hear the cries of hunger and frustration. There was no one head of the household so, in effect, every one was head. Still there was one point in favour of the arrangement. It was my own house. No one could evict me from it. Even if they tried to, I could refuse.

'My heart had by then become immune to the cruel barbs of my co-wives. I also became adept at them. I had no children or other responsibilities. A childless widow does not know the true meaning of compassion. We just go on living. Since we do not die that easily, we have to live.

'I observed all the penances and bowed in front of any lamp that was lit. I have fasted continuously for fifteen days at a stretch. In those days I was known as the "ascetic of Tekke-dath." How soon it all changed! You may now accuse me, saying it was all a charade. You can mock me as much as you like. But, I have one question for all of you. Have you, the guardians of fidelity and morality, ever raised a finger to protect poor women like me, who did not know what life was all about? This world is not ordained for us you say, and so we wander from door to door, seeking the tranquillity which we are made to believe is the boon of the next world. Our desires not subdued, our emotions uncontrolled, we are likely to slip in the face of worldy desire . . . just one such slip and merciless priesthood and righteous justice pick us up and throw us away, into the deep, bottomless pit of hell. Oh God! Is there no redemption for us through Guruvayoorappan Vadakkunathan, Ekadasi Mahatmyam and Pradosham?'

Through the opening of the door, a hot wind rushed out. Was it a sigh, suppressed and crushed for a long time? The band of priests listened, betraying no visible emotion. Were they devoid of even a drop of human feeling? No one wanted to say anything. After a brief silence, the voice continued with greater strength.

'I am not blaming anyone. This is my fate. Aren't there many Namboodiri women who come to listen to the reading of the Epics? Did any of them have such an experience? Every year, even in this temple, such a reading is held. Many Namboodiri women come. We come there not only because we want to hear legends and tales of the Lord but also because there is a desire to get out of our homes, even though we have to cover ourselves with shawls and hide under umbrellas; we come here out of the desire to hear a man's voice, without being seen. Along with these desires, one has the satisfaction of having listened to the Epics and the chanting of prayers offered on such occasions. We can go anywhere without incurring displeasure. The unfulfilled widows, the ill-treated co-wives and the eternal virgins—all of us assembled behind that rice granary. A unity forged out of tears, pain and anguish.

'Our house is adjacent to the outer temple walls, which is very convenient. After the early morning bath and worship we would wait for the reading to begin. What excitment there was! I was reminded of what my grandmother used to say: "When Meppathur and Swamiyar called, the Lord used to appear in front of them. Just think, child, how fortunate one has to be to reach that stage, how blessed even to listen to those people."

'The man who read to us was not an ascetic. Nor was he an old man, who had entered the path of devotion after renouncing all the pleasures of life. When he came in after his bath, wearing a dhobi-washed cloth, with a fresh castemark on his forehead, bookstand in hand, everyone stood up involuntarily. His face had that kind of glow. He sat down cross-legged in front of the bright oil lamp. He must have been about thirty-five years with a fair, sturdy body and wide chest. He wore a yellow dhoti and had flowers from the offerings in his hair. At each stage during the reading, when he lifted his head to explain the text to us, his emotion-filled eyes had the same glow that lit the diamond earrings he wore.

'All of us, Namboodiri women, used to imagine that he was the incarnation of Krishna and we worshipped him. His reading had music, humour and eloquence. Listening to the pranks of the darling young Krishna of Ambadi, a mother who had recently lost her child, burst into tears. Another old woman shed tears of joy when she listened to the episode of the theft of the child and the blessing of the Brahmin women. "Oh Lord Krishna! The protector of devotees!" The wise old women nodded their heads in appreciation, "He may even turn out to be better than Vazhakkunnam."

'I did not find the story of the young cowherd's pranks interesting. What was there to be so enchanted by in the precocious deeds of a child? I did not have a child. Nor was there a possibility that I might. Why should I listen to the narration of that section? I was more interested in looking at the reader than in listening to him.

'By and by the reading reached the chapter on the Ras Leela. I think that this is undoubtedly the best section in the *Bhagavatha*. As the number of women participants increased, the reader's enthusiasm also grew. His eyes opened wide and his words seemed to have a power of their own. He looked as though he was Sri Krishna himself.

'He saw a special significance in the cowherd stealing the saris of the milkmaids. He said that this was the harbinger of the erotic love play Sri Krishna indulged in with a thousand women on the banks of the Yamuna, while their men slept. He explained the meaning of each line explicitly. Listening to these arousing descriptions, the young virgins would bow their heads shyly. The wives would smile. The widows would sigh and remember the old experiences, and then resort to chanting prayers. I did not have any of these emotions. I had no hopes, no experiences. My reaction was one of indifference and detachment. Those emotions were to be stored and kept for the next birth if there was one.

'He was reciting a memorable verse from the *Gopika Gita*, and explaining its meaning.

'Oh! That Radhika was a fortunate woman. Leaving her husband, her children and all her other duties, she succumbed to the lure of that golden flute. She believed that love alone was a refuge and revelled in love play. Oh! Lord Guruvayoorappan, who can fathom your playful dalliances? Sin and virtue, justice and ethics are all mirages. Can a human heart have a greater purpose than that indeterminable intoxication of love? One can ignore the ten incarnations or even the other sections of Sri Krishna's life story. But the universally appealing stories of Vrindavan crossed the barriers of the Yugas and immersed us in a sea of bliss.

'Love is devotion, love is salvation. The attainment of love is the real release and peace.

'I gazed at that face intently, hoping for an explanation, one that was beyond the power of mere words. Love is release, love is happiness, what is the meaning of the fulfilment of love?

'In the auspicious lamp's glow he sat with the open book of *Bhagavatham*, his eyes half closed, his hands joined in prayer. He looked like the very essence of love personified. For one minute his shining eyes looked into the inner room. Only then did I realize that my face was closest to the door. With a tremor, I withdrew my face. I was seized by an unknown emotion, shyness, shame or restlessness, I did not know which. I was afraid. Had he seen me, had he seen my unruly hair and pale cheeks? What an ugly apparition!

'My eldest sister's son had a small mirror. That evening, I took it out secretly and looked at myself. After a long time, my own face loomed in front of me. Was there a hidden beauty in my pale and sorrowful face? Was it like Radha's pale and beautiful face, reflecting the pangs of her separation?

'The next day, after my bath, I remembered to comb my hair. I put a leaf-shaped mark in sandalwood paste on my forehead, instead of the usual mark made with ashes. The garland made of ten flowers, still young and fresh, was tucked into the hair carefully. Then, with my umbrella and the shawl, I went to the temple as usual. In front of the Mandapam I heard someone chanting. The voice was very mellifluous. Moving the umbrella to one side, I glanced at him covertly. He was also looking at me. I was seized by a strange anxiety. My feet faltered. I couldn't see clearly. Without circling the temple once more, I came back.

'After this event, whenever I went for the reading I sat in one of the back rows. I hesitated to look at people's faces. But I couldn't help going for the readings. I derived consolation from listening to those words, and sitting near him. Or was it all on account of the greatness of the Lord's name?

'My thoughts while I slept and ate were all focussed on the banks of the Yamuna, with the blue Kadambas in full bloom. Lovelorn Radha and the amorous Krishna. Who is this that I see, clad in a yellow silk cloth, wearing diamond studs and smiling? Was this how the Lord looked? After all, the Lord can take any shape he wants.

'In the month of *Makaram*, on misty dawns, I would take a dip in the pond and worship at the hour of the first puja. I have been doing this for a long time. When I was young, someone had advised me that it would help to get what my heart desired. I did not have any special desire. Yet I performed this ritual religiously. Recently, while bathing, I heard the chanting of hymns which had a very soothing effect on me in the cool dawn. The waves rippled in the water. Perhaps some other soul was taking a bath—someone lonely like me.

'Even though I felt tired, and I had been fighting with my transient desires, I swear truthfully, that I did not even imagine the events that followed.

'On a moonlit night in *Makaram*, as the pale shadows moved around and created the impression of dawn I hurriedly went to the bathing ghat. I even forgot to call the servant girl who used to accompany me on such trips. I felt it would be a pity to miss the early morning worship. I had just taken a dip in the pond and wiped my body, when I heard the call of the nightingale from the Asoka tree in the courtyard of the temple. The wind was laden with the fragrance of night blossoms.

'As the full moon dipped into the western sky, the shadow of the bathing ghat behind me loomed larger. In between the moonlight and the shadow, there spread before me, the big pond, like a woman's heart, silent and yet suffused with emotion.

'The outline of a poem took shape in my imagination. This night must be like one of those beautiful nights on the banks of the Yamuna. On one side, the peak of the Govardhana mountain, shining in the moonlight with a green silky sheen. A soft breeze playfully captured the rapture of spring. On the other, the village of the cowherds slept in the dark night.

'In between the Kalindi river flowed slowly, reflecting in her tender heart, the blue sky studded with millions of stars, nudging the red and white lotuses to wake up. Centuries ago those banks reverberated with that sweet flute song of divine love. It echoed and re-echoed beyond the barriers of Yugas and even in the present day, even in emotionally barren beings like me, kindled strange hopes and desires.

'Thus, lost in my thoughts, I began to hum the tune of a song from the Asthapadi, that I had learnt in my youth. The human mind is at times unforgivably weak. On some occasions, in some places, one is unable to control onself. Even you mighty men are like that. Then, can you blame this poor Namboodiri woman? Even in this half dazed state of mind, when two warm hands clasped me from behind, in an embrace, I shivered. Who could it be? Was it the Lord himself? Hadn't he suddenly appeared before the devotees like this, many times?

'Waking up from the world of imagination, my own rational mind protested, "No, it is not possible. During the Kali Yuga such an experience is impossible. So, then, who could it be?" The cry which arose from the depths of my soul got stuck at the lips. Someone smothered it with a soft kiss. A fluttering to escape and then the succumbing to a powerful embrace. In that high tide of emotion, the strength to control oneself ebbed away; the awakening of many feelings, many desires hitherto unknown, and unfelt! Perhaps I was tired. But this was not a dream nor sleep. In my fight against nature I, like many others, was in the end, defeated. If that is a sin, I am willing to stake the price of my whole life as the price for that sin.

'Were such meetings repeated? Do not ask me who my beloved was. I am the guilty one. Punish me. No one else is a party to this act.

Translated by Vasanthi Sankaranarayanan
Published in Malayalam as: Kuttasammatam

When Dreams Turn Live

SARAH THOMAS

The *puradam* day had just dawned. Devakiamma was restless. Before the next dawn, a hundred things had to be put in order. Though the steward Raman Nair and the maidservant Sarada were there to help, she had to see to various things herself.

Her children and their families should not want for anything. That had never happened before. Only yesterday morning, when Unni called from Dubai, had it been confirmed that all of them would be with her in their family home for Onam. Letters had already come announcing the arrival of Appu, Sarala and their children, as well as Kesavan, Padmini and their family. There had been some doubt about whether Unni would come. His wife was three months pregnant and had been advised not to travel. And she did not want to insist on their coming. Yet, if Unni was not there when her other two children came and were all together—he was the youngest, the darling who had toddled about, hanging on to the end of her sari . . . when was it? It seemed like yesterday. His growing up, crossing the seas for a job and getting married, all those things had a dreamlike quality even now—if Unni was not around there was no celebration of Onam or the birthday as far as mother was concerned. That had always been the constant complaint of the older children. Anyway, because Rajani's brother had arrived there with his N.O.C. (no objection certificate) looking for a job, the problem had been solved. Unni could now come home in peace. After all, his near and dear ones, this place and Onam, Vishu and the temple festival are all today—indeed, had always been—very important to him till, that is, he got married. Once a year, choosing an auspicious day, he would make it a point to come home. With him came friends and fun. The sleepy house would suddenly be full of life.

All that had changed three years ago. She knew that she shouldn't complain. She should remember that her son was now married. He had his own constraints. The girl had been chosen by her, at his insistence, as a solution to his sadness at leaving her alone in her old age. It was not for gold or money; he only wanted a girl who would be willing to attend on his mother. But, as he went back after his leave, Rajani's face grew dark with sorrow.

Unable to bear this she herself paid for her to go out and join him. Three years had passed. He was coming home for the first time after that.

Appu came only once in five years. He and his family had to spend a huge amount to come from America and then to go back. What's more, it was he who had suggested that all three of them should meet at home once a year during Onam. After all, it was not merely the Onam season. The *Avittam* day of the month of *Chingam* was her birthday too. Yes, she would be seventy after three days. She started reminiscing about her early married life . . . her eyes closed . . . a long moment of oblivion enveloped her. Now, it was his (her husband's) image that appeared before her eyes—busying himself about the yard and cowshed.

Now and then, he called out instructions. Do this, Devoo! Do that . . . three children fit to be stuffed into a single basket. Yet she had never stepped aside in hesitation on a single domestic matter. She had worked along with him, with one child on her hip and the other hanging onto her hand, till she was bone weary. Those had been the times!

All this wealth had been amassed by such hard work,

turning blood into sweat in the process; the two-storeyed house built after demolishing the family house; the coconut grove purchased and the farm-land block of Thekkemanakkel leased—all in the same manner. He could never enjoy leisure, even for an hour. And then? One day as he came back after work, he fell lifeless on the steps like an uprooted tree. Yet, she held out without weakening. The sons he had left her with! Who did they have—other than her—to support them? Hadn't he made enough not only to support the children till they were settled in life but also for them to lead a life of comfort till they died? His presence alone was missing.

So far she had controlled the family affairs with all dignity. She could hold her head high then and now. Valyedathe Devaki Amma (Devoo) still commanded awe and respect. Devakiamma, the owner of a two-storeyed bungalow, coconut groves and paddy fields—her unwillingness to admit that these proud possessions had turned out to be a burden was another issue!

How much time was wasted in futile thoughts! She walked into the kitchen calling loudly, 'Sarada! Hey Sarada!' She knew that of late only when she actually appeared, would the servant girl acknowledge her. Yet . . .

Sarada had just started lighting the fire. She should have swept the courtyard and scrubbed the verandah by now. This girl does not care any more for my instructions. It is high time she was given a warning. But perhaps after the children had come and gone. Otherwise she might pull a long face before them—and all that will irritate the children. They always complained that I was not kind enough to the servants.

Again, her thoughts went back to the preparations for receiving the children. The room upstairs should be made ready for Appu and Sarala. That was the only room he liked in the house. According to him that was the only room with some privacy. He felt that the room downstairs was like a thorough-fare, with everyone going in and out. Rekha and Reshmi could be accommodated in her room, although she felt that they might not like the musty odour there. She had gathered as much from their conversation in English with their father when they came last time. Appu was against the idea of letting them sleep in their parent's room. Letting the children sleep with their parents was unthinkable in America. The next was Kesu and his family. The bedroom was not a big issue here. Even the hall downstairs was enough for them; they lived in a two-roomed flat on the fourth floor of a huge building, on a busy street in Bombay. Kesu's wife though, aping her elder sister-in-law from the United States, pretended to be unhappy with the limited facilities here. She had once hinted that the bedroom used by her and her husband when he was alive could be opened up and given to them. But, Devoo pretended not to hear. Somehow, she loved to keep that room as it was, swept and scrubbed, with a big lamp lit inside it.

For Unni, even the sofa in the drawing-room would suffice. Once he was back here, he had no time to be at home. He would go off in search of his old friends, and would be lost with them in the temple-courtyard or by the river or at the market corner. He would come home only around midnight because he knew she would wait for him and would not eat her food.

After deciding on the rooms, she instructed Sarada to sweep them out, sun the mattresses and make the beds.

The next item was food. The children's tastes had all changed. No one wanted hot, sour or salty things, as before. Curds, curry without a sour taste, sambar without chillies, pickles without salt—she knew that even if the curries were prepared in this manner, they would not please them. It was difficult for them to have even one meal without fish or meat. Still, on an auspicious Onam day! Yes, Onam dishes would do! *Adaprathaman* on Onam day—for the children.

Although she knew that jaggery *payasam* was not generally liked, she was not prepared to change the customs that were part of their lives when he was alive. How delicious was the *Adaprathaman* that he himself used to prepare just to suit the children's palates. Making *adas* with the pounded and finely strained raw rice cultivated in paddy fields on the East side;

then extracting the milk from the juicy and rich coconuts plucked from the special coconut tree and then mixing it with the jaggery made out of sugarcane. His face would glow with satisfaction as the children hungrily licked the last of the *payasam* off the plantain leaf! Oh! Wasn't it better to refrain from conjuring up the memories of the past!

Appu was sure to arrive by the noon train. But he would stay in Sarala's house for one night. That was done with the intention of distributing all the special stuff brought from America to her folks. Their neighbour, Revathy teacher who had now rented the gate-house had told her about it. Appu had never forgotten to present his mother with an *Onapudava* and shawl. Yet when she heard about the gifts that Sarala gave her mother and sisters so lavishly how she missed having a daughter then! He had been very sad about not having a daughter till he died. But in those days she had prided herself over the sons who, when grown up, would be a prop to her— and now she had begun to think in this way—how fickle the mind was!

It was quite late into the night by the time preparations for the children's stay were complete. The huge bronze vessel, scrubbed and polished and filled with water, was kept in the bedroom upstairs. Hadn't they written to inform her that they would be with her in time for breakfast? Appu and Sarala should not have to bother about fetching water for bathing as soon as they came.

As she lay down to sleep, she started mentally ticking off each item to make sure she had not forgotten anything. The three children were going to be in their family home after five years. They should not want for anything, because she was there. As Revathy teacher said, 'Valyamma's daughters-in-law are lucky. Do they have any problems in their husbands' house? Everything goes according to schedule. They only have to sit, stretch their feet and enjoy everything. But I wonder if they realise the value of what they have. When I go to my house on Saturday, my mother-in-law is waiting to go to her daughter's house—my husband has ordered that his mother should be given two days off. She takes care of the house only in name. All the difficult jobs are left for me. Once I go to that house I get time to bathe only after coming back here.'

As Revathy teacher says, it would be interesting to see how these children and daughters-in-law would manage if I was not at home for a day!

As she lay, brooding over many things, sleep overtook her in the early hours of the morning.

In her sleep, she entered a strange world of dreams.

It was just dawn. Raman Nair had already come. Sarada too had followed. Because it was the day the children were to arrive. On the previous day, she had given them strict instructions to come early. Why was Raman Nair trying to insert the key into the keyhole and open the locked door instead of coughing as usual to announce his arrival? Oh! no! it was not only Raman Nair and Sarada, but she too was standing outside the house. Magic!

Imagine! She was not inside the house! Never in the last fifty years had this happened! He had insisted that wherever she went, she should come back home to sleep. She had never tried to violate that principle. And, why had this happened now? Did it mean that she had been removed from the house without any previous warning? It was a moment of weakness! Her thoughts turned into anxiety, which began to intensify. She was hurrying to get inside along with Raman Nair. He was giving some instructions to Sarada. Suddenly, he went to the northern side of the house and yelled out 'Look here! First, clean up Grandma's *Asthithara*. Everything else can be done after that!'

What! Grandma's *Asthithara* ! That meant her own *Asthithara*? Only then did it dawn upon her that she was no more! My God! Now, when the children came home, who would look after their comforts? If only I could let them know how helpless I am after death!

No! Sarada just stood rooted to the ground like a pillar!

'Girl! Why do you stand there and stare?' Raman Nair asked coaxingly. She muttered, twisting her lips, 'Hm! Indeed, I must light the lamp, eh! When alive, did she give us any rest? It was with such difficulty that I saved some money and made a pair of anklets, on the last Onam day! And she did not let me wear them in this house even for a day. Wicked woman! "Maid-servants need not walk about jingling bells, she said".'

What ingratitude! Was it not she who had lent her the thirty rupees because she did not have sufficient money to buy the anklets? She had not paid it back either! Then how can she say I didn't allow her to walk about jingling her anklet bells? She was the one who flirted with everybody, from the milkman who comes in the morning to the Ezhava labourer who comes at dusk to tap the toddy. Then, when Unni was at home—if she was not checked—oh, it was only her private fear this, after all. Never mind! Doesn't Appu say, whenever he comes home, that one should not expect gratitude and love from servants?

Raman Nair was talking to Sarada, patting her on the back consolingly.

'Foolish girl! That's all over! Now what we have to do is to please the old woman's children. Let them go back without any complaint after giving us fifty or a hundred rupees as tips. When the mother was alive, she would never allow them to give us anything even if they wanted to. Now, that nuisance is over.'

Was it the same Raman Nair who was talking like this, cursing her with such hatred? She had never thought of him as a paid employee. He had forgotten all the generosity she had showered at the marriages of his three daughters, and also when he built his house. A sort of depression crept into her mind—there was some truth in what he said. Wasn't it her duty to prevent any wastefulness on the part of her children? Raman Nair did not have the sense to understand these things—didn't he also have grown up children?

But why had all her children taken her absence as a stroke of luck? She had no time to think further. She heard a car stopping at the gate. Sarada was running towards the well with the bucket, 'Oh! I have not kept water on the verandah. And they've come after such a long journey! They'll want to wash and clean their hands and feet before coming inside!' At least she had that much sense.

She stood on the verandah, watching. This was not Appu and his family. It was Kesu, Padmini and the children. And Raman Nair, carrying the boxes and mattresses. The children were grimy with dirt and dust from the two-day long train journey. Why did her son stop silently for a second at the entrance of the house? Is there sadness in his eyes? Perhaps he is remembering me. Poor Kesu! Perhaps my absence is painful for him.

In the next moment Padmini's mocking voice could be heard speaking to Sarada as she began to pour water on her feet, 'Go away, girl! As if I am going to take off my chappals and wash my feet! To please whom? At least now one can have one's way in this house.'.

The daughter-in-law seemed to be talking as though she was relieved. Was my presence such a great problem for her?

Does my son have nothing to say against that? He seems to agree with her. Don't they know that it's not done to take footwear splattered with mud into a scrubbed and clean house? Upto now her anxiety had been confined only to their comforts. But now her mind was sore. She did not even feel like entering the house with them. Let them have everything as they please. Why should I . . . Look! The son was whispering something to his wife. Perhaps it was because she was dead that she could hear everything so clearly. 'You go and tell Sarada to open father's room and arrange it for us. Our married life in Bombay was such a mess with the children always around. Even here it's been the same. At least this time we can have some privacy.'

Was that her son who was talking thus? Was it true that there was so much selfishness tucked away within him? Suddenly, her thoughts became entangled. From his point of view, what he said was true. She could have arranged privacy for them when he came on leave after so many years. Yet at a

time when he should feel grief-stricken over her absence, her
son . . . ! She did not want to hear anything more. She sat
leaning against the parapet wall of the verandah, her hands
covering her ears.

She did not know how long she sat like that. Another sound
at the gate! She stood up in surprise. It was Appu. Who were
those three persons along with him wearing trousers and
shirts? Where were Sarala, Rekha and Reshmi? Or perhaps
they had not come because she was no longer there. They used
to come down from upstairs only to eat. How would it be if
there was no one to prepare or provide food?

Oh! Raman Nair seemed to know those who had come with
Appu. All of them were talking and laughing. Kesi and family
were running down the steps to receive them. She still couldn't
recognize them.

It was Padmini who said, laughing loudly:

'Oh, you look fantastic in pants! If mother was here, she
would not have been able to tell brother-in-law from sister-in-
law or the children.'

What am I hearing? These people in trousers and shirts
with cropped hair are Sarala and her children! Sarala was
heard whispering to Padmini, as they were going inside, 'You
know how comfortable these clothes are. This is what we are
used to. Before this we had to start growing our hair six
months before coming here. I would have to hear all kinds of
rubbish from Mother if I didn't land up here looking like a true
Indian Lady! Last time how strongly she opposed my wearing
a nightie at home! I told Appu that day that I would not enter
this place as long as Mother was alive.

Moreover, in that country it isn't usual to care for the father
and mother. Yet it was all because of Appu's old-fashioned
ways that I came this time, and because of our share in . . .'

She did not have the courage to listen any more. How could
Sarala, who was the mother of two children, bring herself to
speak thus? Did she not know that a similar fate could well
await her? It is true that I objected when she came to drink
bed-coffee wearing something called a 'nightgown', through

which all her undergarments could be clearly seen. Unni was not married then. Kesu had then come home without his family. Moreover, when a person, whom the younger brothers-in-law think of as their mother, appears in such a shameless manner . . . !

Although Padmini had gone upstairs with a long face, she had no idea that that was the moment at which she had decided not to step into this house as long as she was alive. So, wasn't her absence a triumph for Padmini? She had to move away from these loveless daughters-in-law.

She should get into the relative calm of her room with her grandchildren who were born of her blood. Rekha and Reshmi were exploring the room excitedly. Both were equally happy! She couldn't understand what they were saying—it was in English. Still, it was a pleasure to watch them! The eldest girl was fourteen. She didn't look like a girl. She had his face. The broad forehead, sharp nose and thick lips. Even the odd tooth that appeared on the left as she laughed aloud was like his. A pleasant whiff of cool air! When she heard what her granddaughter said to Sarada, who brought milk for the children, she couldn't help sobbing.

They considered it good luck to have got the room to themselves. They said that the foul smell of her medicated oil, her snoring and her choking cough were all disgusting to them. No! She would not stay here anymore. Her grandchildren rejoiced in having got rid of her. She came out with a throbbing heart.

Appu and Raman Nair in the courtyard. Appu was taking all the soda bottles that Raman Nair had brought.

Raman Nair said with a faint smile:

'Now there is no need for you to go upstairs to drink. You can do so in the dining room. I have brought the chicken from my house. You don't have to worry about Mother seeing it.'

Appu was also laughing.

'I remembered it only when Raman Nair mentioned it. Go and ask them to set the table. I shall bring the bottle. Anyway it is very easy now.' When she heard Appu muttering these words to himself she was really shocked. She hadn't expected this from him.

What did he say was easy? Sitting in the lounge and drinking before lunch, or her absence?

She was too weak to think any more. She groped slowly towards the verandah. She sat leaning against the parapet wall. Unni was still to arrive. He would probably come today. Tomorrow was Onam. He wouldn't break the habit of many years. After seeing him once more—

But it was the postman who came in Unni's place. She understood that it was Unni's letter when Raman Nair took it from the postman and went inside. She felt a sudden anxiety to learn of his whereabouts. Had Rajani fallen ill this time? How I long to see a baby born to him. She had made many offerings to God. She waited for the children's discussion of the letter.

Peals of laughter like a string of crackers! What had he written to cause so much mirth? The mounting curiosity to hear it. The children's voices from the lounge—it seems that Rajani was not pregnant at all. What they had written was a lie.

It was all because she was afraid she would have to stay with mother for some days if she came along with Unni, whose nature would demand it of her—they were going on a tour of Europe this year instead of coming to India and getting bored! Unni need not feel guilty this time for disappointing Mother.

Yes, what he wrote was true—a kind of detachment filled her mind. Yes, hereafter not only Unni, but nobody, nobody need feel guilty about me. Suddenly, she felt relieved. I can now withdraw dispassionately from here—from this family turned alien to me . . .

What happened next? Where did I go? No, she couldn't remember anything.

As she opened her eyes, it was really bright. But she did not worry about the hundred things to be supervised. The many splendoured day for which she had been waiting for five years had lost its charm forever. She could only remain lying down, frozen in her confused thoughts, unable to decide whether she was an indispensible or unwanted person in that house.

Translated by Jancy James
Published in Malayalam as: Sandhya Irulum Neram

Granny

SHOBHA WARRIER

Standing outside the post office Patty cried out 'Ayya!' Her voice was filled with fear. She called again, tremulously,

'Ayya!' Arumukham, the postman, heard her this time.

'Who is it? Patty! Where have you been this last one week? We thought you were dead.' Arumukham laughed as though he had cracked a joke. Everyone looked up on hearing Arumukham's laughter.

'Really, Arumukham, have you gone mad? How can you speak to poor Patty like this? Patty! . . . Where were you for one week?' said Subramoni.

'It is not I . . . but you who have gone mad . . .' Arumukham was becoming angry. Subramoni continued to sort letters, ignoring him.

'Where is Ayya, Kanna?' Patty asked, standing hidden behind the door.

'Ayya hasn't come yet, Patty. He must be at home. You can look for him there,' Subramoni said in a kind voice, without looking up.

'Muruka! My Lord,' invoked Patty, and squatted on the floor. She had not come to sweep the post office for a whole week. But she felt they would all laugh if they found out why. Which is why she didn't offer any explanation.

On Saturday, Patty was returning after filling water in the

earthen pot. She had barely walked a furlong from the gate. She does not remember clearly what happened after that. She only knows that she hit against something and fell down. It was only later that Patty understood that she had collided with a goat who was standing in the middle of the road. So forceful was the collision that she had been flung onto the ground, and even though someone came along and tried to help, she fell down again, unable to sit up.

'Patty, can't you see? See what happens when you go and hit against goats on the wayside.'

It was a long time since cataract had begun to trouble Patty. Her vision had been fading day by day. Now she saw things only in a sort of blur. Once Patty said to Saravanan that she had been told by Subramoni, an employee in the post office that cataract could be cured with an operation. 'An old woman, doesn't need to see more than this,' chided Saravanan and Saivamuthu in unison. Neither of them, Patty's grandchildren, were interested in spending money on an operation for an old woman who might die any day.

Every day, Patty used to get up before sunrise. She could tell the time of the day exactly without looking at the clock. It was the talk of the post office. Subramoni would ask Patty the moment he saw her: 'What time is it now, Patty?' 'Why Kanna! Are you asking me this to tease me?', Patty would enquire, displaying her toothless gums in a broad smile. After that she would tell him the time. Subramoni's question and Patty's reply could be heard several times a day.

Seeing Patty's smile, Venkitakrishnan would express his doubts about any teeth being left in Patty's mouth at all. She would reply in the affirmative, 'of course'. And then open her mouth, to show one or two molars reddened from chewing. Everyone would laugh at her and ask,' are these teeth?'

'Can't you see me chewing up the betel leaves and areca-nut? My only wish is that I should have at least one tooth to chew betel leaves till I die,' Patty lamented with a long sigh.

'Patty! You cannot chew with just one tooth!' Arumukham would say, laughing loudly.

Subramoni liked to ask, 'How old are you, Patty?' At times Patty would say that she was twenty, at other times sixty and at times even a hundred! And everyone would laugh at these answers. At first Patty did not understand why they laughed, and she would also join in that laughter, without realising that she was the butt of their jokes. 'Do you know why we laughed?' Subramoni would ask.

'I don't want to know. You wouldn't be mocking or ridiculing me, would you?' Patty would say, laughing innocently.

Patty's Kanna (darling), that is what others, especially Arumukham, called Subramoni. Patty loved Subramoni more than her own life.

There was a reason for this. Subramoni gave her the love that neither her own grandchildren nor the strangers in the post office bestowed on her. Patty's daughter-in-law, the mother of Saravana and Saivamuthu, often ranted, 'Damnation! Why doesn't this old crone die! Spitting hard into the courtyard and raising her hands high she would curse: 'Go kill yourself, old woman!' Patty would then sit silently in a corner of the courtyard, smeared with cowdung. Her daughter-in-law would go on swearing: 'Oh! this cursed woman, born to consume everything, won't die! I would have killed and buried her long ago but for the hundred rupees she brings. Saravana! Give her a kick. Let's be rid of the old woman!'

Why haven't I become deaf? If only it was my ears that were blocked instead of cataract in the eyes! Patty would close her eyes and pray to Lord Muruka: 'It is my fate that I should have to hear all this. Lord Muruka! Why don't you take this old woman away?', Patty would say loudly. Then tears would stream down from her white cataract-filled eyes.

The severest pain came when she was confined to bed, having sprained her leg, by knocking against the goat. There was no one to hold her and take her into the compound. She fell down on the floor several times, unable to bear the pain that shot through her feet as she stood up. Patty believed that she was cured of all that because of Lord Muruka's mercy.

Patty thought of the good old times lying curled up on a

threadbare mat on the floor. How long ago that was! Her father had given her in marriage with a chain, big earrings and nose-rings, a brocade sari and bronze vessels. Her man sold the chain, nose-rings, and earrings, one after the other. Patty proudly remembered how her man was different from the other men in the neighbourhood, even though he used to steal everything and drink toddy. He had never beaten Patty, not even once. He gave up all his savings to the toddy shop. Nevertheless, late at night, however drunk he might be, he would come home with a packet in each hand—a jasmine garland in the small leaf-packet and idlis in the bigger one. As soon as he entered the house he would wake his sleeping wife, calling out, 'My sweetheart'. Then he would arrange the jasmine garland in her hair. Placing the other packet before her, he would say, 'Eat some idli.' As Patty ate the idli half asleep, he would inhale the scent of the jasmine-flowers, sitting behind her. In between, he would speak aloud various dialogues from the cinema: 'You are my life!' 'You are my own!' 'You are my darling!' Patty trembled with joy as she recalled those days. When her heart was filled with sorrow, Patty would think about her man and relive those memories, trying to forget everything.

'See what a skeleton I have become—I who used to be a brown beauty then,' Patty thought, looking at her wrinkled hands and legs. When her man died, Patty's good days also came to an end. In those days, she used to wear a blouse and sari. Now she had no blouse. Just one sari. On the day she washed that blue sari, she got another one from her daughter-in-law only after repeated begging.

Patty could not see the glass pieces lying on the road after she developed cataract. She stepped on the broken glass once or twice. It wounded her feet, which became infected. It was after that that she bought herself a pair of slippers. She was fearful when she handed over the balance from the hundred rupees, after buying the chappals. The daughter-in-law roared like a lion at Patty who stood aside trembling with fear: 'You crone, where is the rest of the money?'

'I bought chappals,' Patty's voice was not audible. Saravanan and her daughter-in-law did not give her food that night. They told her that she need not enter their house if she brought one paise less than a hundred rupees. That day, and many times later, Patty was vexed with the thought that everybody had forgotten that that house belonged to her man. She wept till daybreak; she prayed to Lord Muruka: 'Please take me away too.' Muruka did not hear that pathetic cry.

Patty's job entailed not just sweeping the floor in the post office, but also filling the earthern pot with water and placing it in the office. Sometimes, people would take a drink of water and leave the pot, as well as the glass, lying on the floor. As she swept the floor, squatting on her haunches with head bent, Patty could not see them. The broom hit the earthen pot which toppled over and broke; the room was filled with water. Only Arumukham scolded her, the others consoled her. In less than two days, Patty broke one more pot. As she was coming in with the pot filled with water, she missed a step and fell. That day the Postmaster asked her, 'Can't you see at all, Patty? How will you work?'

Ayya, I will sweep nicely. Excuse me this time.' Patty fell at his feet and wept. Subramoni could not bear the sight. He quickly lifted her up. 'I won't rest until I have cured Patty's eyes.' The others laughed. Patty knocked against a goat after that, and was laid up for a week.

'What, Patty? Where have you been for a week?.' enquired the Postmaster.

'Oh! I went and knocked against a goat because I could not see properly. Now I am all right. Shall I come and sweep tomorrow?' The Postmaster laughed loudly as though he was listening to a joke. As his laughter died down, he said, 'Patty don't you think you've become a bit sickly now? I have asked somebody else to come and work from tomorrow.'

'Oh! Sir, please don't say that! I shall do everything carefully.' Tears flowed profusely from Patty's eyes.

'No, Patty. You'd better go and rest again . . . You have to stop one day . . .' The Postmaster went into his room, laughing.

Patty felt her feet weakening, her vision fading, and her neck being crushed by somebody. Although she wanted to cry out, 'Muruka! Save me!' her voice failed her.

Translated by Jancy James
Published in Malayalam as: Patti

The Fisherman

B. SARASWATHY

Full of hope Kalyani raised the little fishing net with the tip of the long bamboo reed. But even before she spread the net she despaired of seeing the catch. There were no fish in it. She shook the net out on the ground praying the while for at least a minnow. But there was none. Nothing alive was trapped in her little net.

'My God, it is already dusk. And not even a solenette. This is the end for me,' she muttered to herself even as she swung the net over the water again. Taking a little bran mixture from a coconut shell container, she threw it over the net and waited impatiently. She knew the fish wouldn't get into the net that fast. Yet she hoped. The last ray of hope. She prayed to the gods by all their names pleading for at least one fish. She would get one. Certainly she would. What if she didn't? She grew fearful. She felt that her body couldn't take his blows any more. She cursed fate that she had to live with such a man. But was it only fate? Was it not also her fault that things had come to such a pass? She could have said that she was not willing to marry. But nobody had asked for her consent. She had been able to see him before the marriage and had felt that never before had she seen a more unkempt man. And yet she heard the rest of the household say: 'It's the girl's good luck. The boy has a little plot of land and no responsibilities at home.' Yes, she was lucky and did not wish to reject that luck. Nor did she have the courage. And then marriage was a promise of fun. There would be the feast, the hustle and bustle, the new clothes with gold brocade, the chain and the *tali*. All that was good.

It was on the wedding night that she first thought about him. He came to her reeling drunkenly. She screamed in terror. In that black revolting face rolled reddened eyes. She looked at him only once. He tripped over the steps and fell down and started vomiting. She fled, holding her nose against the stench. Somebody came and lay him down properly and cleaned the place. She spent the night sobbing. Even in her worst nightmares she had not imagined such a terrible drunkard for a husband. Oh, why recollect all that now? It was all over wasn't it?

She took some more bran mixture and threw it into the water. She thought how different her experiences were when she had a good catch and when she didn't. He wouldn't eat if there was no fish. And if the food wasn't satisfactory he would beat her, break the vessels and hurl the rice and the plate at her face. Then he would do anything that occurred to him. If the meal was good his mood would be different, that day he would be very affectionate to his wife. He would sit beside her when she ate the remains of his meal. He would utter endearments to her and delight her with erotic songs he had picked up at the toddy shop. She believed that in truth he loved her. If she couldn't cook for him as he pleased he certainly had the right to give her a beating or two. Was it not her duty to satisfy him somehow? She knew this well enough.

Before and after her work in the fields she would spread the net in that still canal. As she pulled the net out, golden and silvery fish would spring about in it. She would catch them all and put them in a pot of water out of reach of dogs and cats. Only then would she eat the gruel of rice and water. In this way, without much effort, she could provide a curry.

There had been other occasions as well when she had not caught any fish. At such times she would invariably make up for the lack by getting fish from elsewhere. Once or twice she borrowed from Paru on the other side of the canal. Since she had had luck on some days Paru had been only too eager to lend. Kalyani had to clear the debt only when she had a good catch. Sometimes she would buy from those who fished with big nets on the canal bank. But they would not give on loan. Neither did they want fish in return. They wanted only money. This Kalyani did not like. She had no such item as 'money' in her budget. And yet she often had to part with money to buy fish. The small savings she had in her little earthern pot would be reduced by a few coins. She hoped that one day when she had a beloved little son, the pot would grow full.

Kalyani felt that she had made a bad start that day. Even if she was willing to part with a few coins from her savings, there were no fishermen on the river bank. She had picked a quarrel with Paru over some coconut palm leaves. Paru might have caught some fish but Kalyani could not ask her for any. In truth Paru had been the cause of the quarrel. But people believed that Kalyani was to blame. Kalyani had seen a palm leaf drop from the coconut palm on her land. But Paru had used a stick to drag the palm leaf out of the water, where it had fallen and had taken it home. Was it her fault that Kalyani had picked a quarrel? Was it wrong of her to have called Paru a liar? But Paru had not given in. She had hurled at Kalyani all the choicest abuses that she could think of. Hearing the quarrel their respective husbands had arrived on the scene. Both vowed vengeance for the abuses flung at their wives. The women blew their noses and walked into their thatched huts. The verbal exchange was now between the men. They stood on either bank of the canal and furiously threatened to cut and stab each other, to slice each other into bits and to fling the bits into the canal. It took the efforts of the local bigwigs to quieten them down. And after all that, how could she now ask Paru for fish? She wouldn't even think of it. If this time she could get at least two little fish she would be able to tide things over.

She raised her net with a prayer. There was a glittering fish thrashing about in it. Though not very big, it wasn't that small either. Her face glowed. She laughed without meaning to.

It was when she turned to shake out the net that she saw a young man approaching at a distance. Seeing the stranger she blinked in surprise. Her joy at having got a fish had brought a fullness to her lips and a glitter to her eyes. She blinked. She could not recognise the man. And yet she felt that she had seen him somewhere. Where was it? She skipped through her memory. Oh, she realised . . . in the *Ramayana*! A figure like that of Srirama in the *Ramayana*. He had no tuft of hair on the back of his head, no drape of bark (*valkalam*) and no sacred thread. But he had a bow and arrow. She knew that the object tied to his wrist was for telling the time. She had seen others before with similar objects tied to their wrists. That handsome face and figure was like that of Srirama. The large bow and arrow! That object called a catapult was used for fishing. Kalyani had seen many others before with a catapult but she had never felt that any of them were like Srirama. This man did not belong to the locality. She was sure of everyone around here. Most of the people here were known: those who worked on the farms and those who employed the farm labourers. She could recognise all those who worked with her. Besides, it was not difficult for her to understand that the man belonged not to the class of labourers but to the class that employed them. But there were no employers thereabouts whom she didn't know. It must be someone who came from far away. Oh, let him be anyone!

'Look, the fish has escaped,' said the young man who had by then come close to her.

She was shocked. 'Oh, I've been cheated,' she exclaimed. She shook out the net. No, the fish was not to be seen. It had escaped. In the distant west, near the edge of the earth the sun God glowed like a red ball of fire. She gazed at Him in despair. He caressed her affectionately, dabbed her pale face with red paint. The soft breeze danced through her dry curls. The young man stood gazing in delight at the poetic vision before him. She turned to look, not at him but at the heavy fish as big as small winnowing seives, that hung from the hooks he carried.

'Are these for sale?' she asked not looking at his face but rather addressing the fish.

'Yes,' he replied smiling. 'Your catch has escaped, hasn't it?' He threw down the heavy fish that he was carrying before her. The wretched creatures were thrashing about on the string that was drawn firmly through their mouths. Their eyes stared. Kalyani felt sympathetic towards them though her own sorrow was above theirs. Today her husband might beat her to death. These fish were expensive. Otherwise she would have bought one.

'How much does one cost?' she asked looking gravely at the seller. But on seeing his face she hung her head shyly.

'The three small ones are one rupee each. These two are one and a half rupee each.'

'Oh, why do you want four times the price? Ask a reasonable price. It is getting dark.'

'Is it my fault that it is getting dark? I mentioned a reasonable price. You may buy if you wish!'

'No, I don't want . . . Oh, it is night already! When shall the rice be cooked?' Muttering thus half to the stranger and half to herself Kalyani picked up her things and started walking.

'You haven't mentioned what price you are willing to give,' he called out to her.

She turned round and said, 'You will not lower the price, will you?'

'Stop and hear me.' Taking the fish the man went up to her and asked, 'How many do you want?'

'A small one. Tell me the price first!'

'Why make it a small one? Have these big ones.' He unhooked the two large fish, strung them separately and held them out to her. She took them. How heavy they were!

'Oh! These will be costly. We aren't that rich,' she said coyly.

'But there is no price on them. I do not catch fish to sell them. I do it for fun.'

'If you are giving them as charity I do not want them.'

'Oh no! They are not for nothing. I shall ask for a price later. For now you may take them.'

He looked at her as if he certainly intended to extract the price of fish. She felt a stab through her heart. She suddenly remembered: night was drawing in. The stars had already come out. She ran.

Kalyani began to cook quickly. The rice and curry should be ready before her husband arrived. Her hands were shaking when she cleaned and cut the large fish. The fish-bones pricked her at places. Her heart was seething even then. What a piercing look! She felt that the staring eyes of the fish were looking at her. She became angry. She prised out the eyes and threw them away. The scales, like silver coins, looked at her gesture and smiled.

Her work was over. The fish was cooking on the fire. She did not think of her husband who would begin eating without enquiring where it had come from. Neither did she feel happy to think that today he would be happy. She thought of the fisherman. Who could he be? How did he trust her enough to give her the fish? 'It is not for nothing. I shall ask for a price.' What did that mean? That look! When she thought of that the wound in her heart bled again.

The master of the house arrived, thus putting an end to her thoughts. The stench of liquor spread around. It was with great difficulty that he stumbled in.

'Hey, you, Kalyani, serve me rice,' he slurred. He sat down, swerving from side to side.

Kalyani served the rice. The steam rose from the rice and curry.

'Where did you get this *karimeen* from?

'Ha! What flavour!' he said, gulping down the food. Kalyani had moved away. He couldn't be trusted till he had finished eating.

'From where did you get this? Speak.'

'I bought it.'

'Good woman. So you have money with you? But when I asked you today you didn't give me any. From where did you

buy the fish?' He ate and asked the questions without expect-
ing any reply from her. Now and then he would spit out the
rejected food that he burped up.

'I bought it from the fishermen with big nets.' After she
spoke, Kalyani realised that she need not have told a lie. It
made no difference to her husband whatever she said. Yet she
was afraid to mention that fisherman even when her husband
was in a drunken state.

He was eating in great swallows, enjoying the taste. Kalyani felt sympathetic towards her husband. Though he was a
drunkard, how much he trusted her! The wound caused by
that fisherman's stabbing look bled again.

After the master of the house had finished eating, the *dhar-
mapatni* (dutiful wife) sat down to eat the remains on the plate.
She ate the rice on it and began to get up.

'Oh, have you finished? Eat well. Finish that curry,' he said.
Her palette forbade her to eat the slices of fish. It was fleshy
meat, like human flesh.

'I don't feel hungry today.' She rose and left.

Kalyani unrolled the mattress, spread it in a corner and
curled up on it. He began singing and dancing. He was not
pleased to see that she was ready to sleep so early on this
happy day. When he saw that she had no intention of getting
up, he pulled her up roughly by the hand. She trembled.

'Ha! What torment is this! A man must learn to hold his
drink. Disturbing others . . .

'Torment . . . who is tormenting? Do you dare to raise your
tongue?' he pushed her. Her head hit the floor. She did not
scream. He stamped heavily on her body with stumbling feet.
Even then she thought not of his cruelty nor of him, but of the
loaded words and glances of the fisherman. She could not
sleep. Whenever she closed her eyes the vision of the stranger
rose before her.

Kalyani did not rise with the dawn. She dozed off a little.
Her husband shook her awake. She who had to warm up
something to eat and then go to work, how could she sleep?

When he saw her he was frightened. There was clotted

blood on her face and hands. Her face and eyelids were swollen and ugly.

'What's the matter, Kalyani?' he asked lifting her up lovingly. He felt grieved, How cruel he had been! Never before had it happened thus . . . once or twice he had hit her and that too had been in a state of drunkenness. Never had there been such obvious marks.

He brought a pot of water and told her to wash her face. He himself lit the fire in the oven and began to cook the rice.

They sat together and ate the rice gruel. She looked at him gratefully and he looked at her with love and repentance. In that silence they communicated eloquently.

Kalyani went to work that day though he had told her she need not. She worked briskly, careless of her bruises, thinking only of her loving husband. Occasionally there arose in her mind the figure of a fisherman . . . the young woman knew that today also the man would come her way.

That evening, as soon as she returned home after work she went directly to the pot in which she kept her savings. Shaking it out she took the half and quarter coins and added to them the half rupee she had in the folds of her dhoti, thus making it three rupees. She walked straight to the bank of the canal. She looked around but didn't see anyone. Spreading her net in the water she waited. Then he came. Today too he carried fish. She bit her lip hard and stood waiting, looking at him. He wore a smile as he approached. When he came close she held out to him the money she carried.

'What are you giving me?'

'The money.'

'Didn't I say that I don't need any money? Today I have only two fish. Here this fellow jumped away twice.'

'Take this.'

'Which of these do you want? Or why not have them both?'

'If you don't need the money. . . there. . . throw it into that canal!'

She threw the money at his feet, proudly turned her head and walked away gravely. A shadow fell over his face.

That day too the husband beat up the wife because the meal was not satisfactory. Though she sobbed for some time she slept well that night.

The next morning they sat together and ate the rice gruel arguing agreeably over whether the new farmer at the farm they worked on was better or worse than the previous one.

Translated by Rohini Ramachandran
Published in Malayalam as: Minkaran

The Soil that Grows Diamonds

K. SARASWATHI AMMA

Drenched to the waist by a huge wave, Neelakantan Nair, who had been standing with his back to the sea, woke up from his meditation on beauty. With his eyes still fixed on the blue sari-clad figure who was walking towards him, he moved back to the shore, wringing out some of the water.

She came a little nearer. As her face became visible, the worshipper of beauty exclaimed to himself: a gem that should adorn the crown of the conqueror of the world!

She was about to pass him by when she raised her head and chanced to glance at him. Stopping abruptly, she asked in great amazement: 'Oh! Neelakantan Chettan?'

For a moment Neelakantan Nair was perplexed. He wondered which of the buds he had known had blossomed into this beautiful flower. 'Is it Saradakutty? My God! Had you taken part in an international beauty competition, you would have won the first prize. I was just wondering who this gem was!'

'Not gem, but I am the earth which produces the gem.' He found the glow of happiness missing in her smile.

'Are you alone?' he asked.

'No, there is an escort. How long has it been since I saw you, Chetta? You have not even cared to cast a glance at us after going away from here!'

'Would it have been of any use, if I had done so?' he said apologetically. 'So far, I have had time only to wander about those places where my father worked or where I studied. Now after father's retirement all of us have settled down in our home-town. So I took this opportunity to come here. Is everyone well at home?'

'They're all fine; no disease, no penury. About four years ago we had a series of misfortunes. Just after my father recovered from fits, he became bed-ridden with paralysis. The only income was the money my little brother received for working as a picker in some tennis court. We suffered quite a bit with no one to help and no means to raise even a few paise. At last there was a way out in a strange form . . . but forget that! How are things in your house? . . . and Nalini?'

'Somehow we managed to find a man for her.' The relief of having unloaded a heavy burden showed on his face. 'What hardship! If the boy is unemployed, we have to find a job for him. If he is employed, solid cash has to be given. Yet, there is no security regarding a girl's future despite what we may give her. Nalini got a husband because we helped him get a transfer from his department.'

'And Visalakshy?'

'She is the next burden. You know how good she is at her studies! But mother thinks that there is nothing more shameful for women than going to work. Doesn't she realize that there is nothing more humiliating than chasing males, trying to catch them like this? What problems! Mother says she will offer me in exchange. But who will she exchange for getting bridegrooms for the remaining four girls? The misery of having daughters!'

The general complaint about womankind produced a painful smile on Saradakutty's lips, and momentarily increased the sorrow in her eyes. With an enigmatic expression she said, 'Don't talk like that, Chetta. Sometimes, when there is no other way out it is possible to redeem everyone by making use of a woman.'

Neelakantan Nair continued to stare at her with wonder and joy, without trying to understand what she was saying. The power of her beauty had immersed him in some day-dream, making him forget his mother's appeal to find a husband for Visalakshy. Saradakutty turned and looked behind her, and then sat on the sand and asked: 'Don't you want to see my daughter?'

Neelakantan Nair felt as though something crystal-like broke within him. Although his hopes of the moment were shattered, he consoled himself that at least he was able to take in that beauty. Seeing a dark young man bringing a curly haired, plump and fair child, he asked her, pale-faced: 'The child's father . . . ?'

'He has gone to see someone urgently.'

'Then who is this?'

Saradakutty turned around. Looking with a sardonic smile at the hefty fellow who was carrying the baby effortlessly she said: 'That's our driver. He resembles the father only in his colouring. How many harmful comforts can those with excessive money afford to buy and destroy their health as well!'

Neelakantan Nair continued to gaze first at the mother, then at the daughter. He realized then that not only did she have the treasure of beauty, worthy of lighting up a feudal lord's home but also the pompousness of the wealthy. He did not feel surprised at that either. He also guessed that the misdeeds of her husband hurt her more than his lack of good looks. For quite some time he did not feel like talking to her about anything. At last he said, 'The baby is the spitting image of you, Saradakutty. When she comes of age, her father will not have to run about to find her a husband.'

'I cannot even imagine him running about. You should see that body! You will wonder how he walks!'

Her tone and expression surprised him. He did not comprehend many things; nor did he know how to ask her about them.

More than the mother's beauty, it was the baby's loveliness that fascinated him. He took the baby from her and covered her with kisses. The baby smiled, showing not even the slightest embarrassment in finding herself in unfamiliar hands. Seeing that, a sigh escaped her, and her eyes became misty. Her baby was unlucky: she had not had the good fortune to see her own father even though there were plenty of other men who gave her affection.

With the baby in his lap Neelakantan Nair sat on the sand and asked, 'Where do you live?'

Believing the question to be posed out of a fondness for the baby, she said, 'She stays with my father and mother. Don't you know our old house? A new two-storeyed building has been constructed in its place.'

'And where do you live?'

'We have settled in Madras. Yesterday was my grandfather's sixtieth birthday. We came down for that. But we are not staying at home. Since one of his good friends and family stay at the Hotel Seashell here, he likes to stay there too. I go over to my house every morning and bring the baby here. Before it gets dark, she is sent back again.'

'It is great that the mother has at least that much love for her daughter!' He felt, for an instant, an excessive affection for the baby who was denied maternal love, and a bitter contempt for the mother who did not perform her duty.

Saradakutty took some time to respond. 'When one realizes what the father wants is not the daughter but only her mother—the mother's body—isn't it proper to oblige?' She quickly corrected herself and said, 'I should not utter such thankless words. He had promised me that he would arrange for a governess and provide other facilities to bring up the baby. But I did not want her to grow up near me, and entrusted her to my mother. I went back to him just three months after the delivery.'

With extreme contempt and hatred he said, 'Won't having babies destroy the mother's beauty?'

'Yes.' she replied in a very serious tone. 'After buying an object and paying its price anyone would be careful to use it with care so as not to cause it any damage. A commodity cannot have any purpose other than that of satisfying the purchaser.' Her expression and tone surprised Neelakantan Nair. He asked, 'Why do you speak in this strange manner?'

'Everything about me has come to assume a strange manner,' she said with a bitter laugh. 'Tell me, brother. How many women do you know who have become a man's property, having bowed and received a bundle of notes in place of the *pudava* from him?'

The expression on his face, which had been one of surprise, now changed. She continued to question him, 'Answer this question too: How many girls have you seen, who are wives of men older than their grandfathers? Many people indulge in fault-finding and condemnation but I have seen the depths of hypocrisy in such people. Yet, I have a consolation. Many can be saved by using my life.' He was unaware that the baby had climbed off his lap onto the sand and was picking up shells. In amazement and disbelief he asked, 'Do you mean to say that you were sold to save the family from penury?'

'Yes! Why are so you amazed? You should compliment me for having achieved so much with my body. There were days when we could not give even rice water to father. Mother had reached the full term of her pregnancy. In those days a *vaidyan* who used to preach about virtuous deeds and mutual help, stayed near our house. A well-known social reformer. I did not then understand the intention behind his offer of all help to us when we needed it, if I was sent to his house. At first father and mother did not agree to this. How many are there of that kind? Nobody values good character or beauty. Only money is important. At last we too adopted the same policy. My mother's family pride got subsumed by poverty and hunger. Mother perhaps felt that it was extremely fortunate that she had a fourteen-year old daughter.'

She stood up, and looked at the horizon where the sun had half set. 'You know, in what plenty father and mother live today! Although I did not get a husband I got a good owner! Compared to other trades this one is heavenly. I consider myself very lucky that though he had his own children to love and care for, he granted me the time and opportunity to have a child of my own. Do slaves have the freedom to maintain relationships with their families, and to visit several places without being suspected? Because one is required to please only one person, the risks and illnesses are very few. How different the situation would be if one went about the other business!'

Stunned, he stared at her. He wondered if the condition of women had become so pitiable that even those with such sweet faces discussed the business of prostitution.

Saradakutty helped the baby to stand up, and wiped the sand off her little hands. Then, smilingly, she asked Neelakantan Nair, who sat there stunned and speechless. 'Why don't you say something, Chetta? I cannot stay here longer. After leaving the child in my home, if I don't reach his place before he arrives, the son will tell his father all kinds of lies. So great is the son's hatred—or love—towards me. The son thinks that he has a better claim on me than the father, at least on account of his age. I don't know what might happen if I decide to talk to his father about this matter.' Still, Neelakantan Nair was silent. How casually she talked about illicit relationships, which no man ever dared to imagine! She read his mind. Bending down and lifting up the baby, she said, 'Even if I suffer because of all this, at least my daughter will be able to live comfortably and decently. I am thinking of adopting a poor child to have a companion for her. Otherwise social reformers with their speeches might perhaps start surrounding her with an eye on her beauty, and wealth.'

Saradakutty turned back and started walking. Neelakantan Nair who had been sitting stunned until then, now got up abruptly, as though shocked out of sleep, and asked her: 'Who is your husband?'

'Not husband, but owner,' said Saradakutty with a burning smile. 'Have you heard of a caste known as the Nattukkottachetti? Our neighbours call those belonging to it Maravan. According to the physician whom I told you about a while ago, my husband is a Kasimaravan (dark maravan). Does it matter what he is? Isn't it enough if my affairs are managed without my having to toil, like someone who is public property?'

Neelakantan Nair went on looking silently in the direction in which she had gone. He felt amazed and detached about the fact that such unusual beauty and goodness had to be sold in the marketplace of pleasure without being received into the sacred institution of marriage. A burning sensation rose in his chest as he thought about his four unmarried sisters.

Translated by Jancy James.
Published in Malayalam as: Ratnamvilayunna Bhumi.

The Stone Woman

K.B. SREEDEVI

When did I last come this way? A long time ago perhaps. . .

My father was with me at the time. But, I did not, while travelling through the skies, see the full beauty of the Earth. Yet, my father who could read my face, would often instruct the pilot to reduce our speed whenever we flew over a holy river or a hermitage. I could smell the fragrance that arose from the sacrificial pits prepared by the sages, as the fresh paddy, ghee and other sacrificial offerings were cooked.

When did it all happen?

A thousand years ago? After that, she had changed. Her life itself had taken a different path.

Or, had it?

Time had changed, but not Ahalya.

She walked ahead. The flowering forest. The spring forest laden with flowers. Flowers strewn everywhere, like a carpet spread encircling the roots hanging from the branches of trees. An illusion of a continuing rain of flowers, created by the sun's rays filtering through the branches.

This time her husband had not raised any objection when she had told him of her wish to attend the final auspicious rituals performed by Sage Valmiki to break his penance. He merely asked her to convey his salutations to the great sage, a devotee of Sri Rama.

In the olden days she wouldn't have been allowed to wander alone in this forest. Nor would she have had the courage to do so.

But today her husband did not doubt her. Nor did she feel afraid. She had gone to him to get his permission to go on this journey. He had placed both his hands on her bowed head and blessed her. Peace be with you. Could this change in him be attributed only to the changing times?

Sri Ramachandra had freed the forest from all demons. Human beings had nothing to fear. It was Sri Rama who taught her not to fear anything other than non-observance of one's own duties. He had given this advice to her when she spoke to him in wonder about his might, which had vanquished demons such as Khara, Dushana and Trisira in a mere three and a quarter hours.

Spiritual strength was indeed greater than physical strength. For a person who had spiritual strength, one quarter of a minute was more than enough to kill fourteen thousand evil forces.

One could go on listening to that voice which resonated like the peal of temple bells. The moment she saw him she knew that her long penance had not been in vain.

She was drowned in the heavenly pleasure evoked by his gentleness.

'Ahalya, I can see your true soul. Wake up from this wordly sleep.'

Why is a sage incapable of uttering such words?

Is it because they have mastered the art of the all-destructive curse?

Ahalya trembled for a moment. How could she blame the virtuous?

At once she corrected herself.

Could she forget the great Valmiki, who was also a sage? Even the curse he uttered, though powerful, was a temporary outburst, arising from an incomparable compassion.

Ahalya tarried for a moment or two in the same place. In

truth, it was not a curse at all. It was the expression of a far-sighted vision.

Even at that time, that sage must have been aware of Sita, the great sacrificial fire. He might also have realised that it was imperative to protect that fire from the indifference and insults of the world, and keep it burning, for the preservation of the human race itself. That was why he . . . .

Ahalya looked at her arms, one after the other. She was shaking with excitement.

Was it surprising? Which woman wouldn't feel proud and excited at the thought of Sita?

Ahalya walked further. The whispers and bird calls of the forest sounded pleasant to her.

Her own past life opened the doors of her mind and looked out.

Hadn't she always felt the same way, this awareness of the changing seasons, the sights and sounds she saw and heard?

All births and deaths seen through naked eyes, unshielded by any curtain!

All those years, she kept wondering, who was more compassionate?

Her husband, who gave her a chance to experience all that. . . .

Or . . . ?

One scene stood out clearly in Ahalya's memories. She was, at that time, living in Gautama's hermitage, experiencing the love and cruelty of nature.

One day, as she stood with her head bowed, after worshipping the early twilight according to the prescribed rituals, she overheard a conversation from somewhere close by. Both the voices belonged to women. She recognised that they were people of Mithila, from their dialect and manner of speech. They had come to pick a rare flower, called lavanyakam, which was available only in Gautama's hermitage.

The younger of the two women asked, 'Why is our young mistress so fond of this flower?'

The answer was, 'Don't you know? She has been told that the worship done with this flower will give her her husband's love. This plant has been brought down from Heaven and nurtured by Ahalyadevi.'

'These days the young mistress is absorbed in prayer and worship all the time.'

'Isn't that natural? Haven't you heard of the arrival of the pair of Krouncha birds who predicted that Sri Rama, the son of King Dashratha will wed Sita?'

'Oh, How lucky! It is indeed the good fortune of the whole of Mithila.' Keeping the flower basket down, she folded her hands and bowed her head in worship.

'After that, the young mistress's mind has been completely absorbed in Sri Ramachandra. She is eagerly awaiting his arrival.'

'Haven't you collected a basketful of flowers?'

'Let us go back. Even now, I feel very sad when I stand here.'

'Why? Why do you feel sad when you are in such a beautiful place?'

'The hermitage seems very empty without the presence of Ahalyadevi.'

Then, there was no word from either of them.

After some time, the voice of the younger person asked, 'Why was Ahalyadevi subjected to such a scandal, even though she was a virtuous woman?'

'Shut up. What are you saying?' The voice of the older woman was filled with anger. 'Ahalyadevi was not born out of a woman's womb, and she is noted for her generosity. Do we really know whose fault it was?'

'Come, let us go. Please remember that we are holding sacred flowers to be used for worship. Let them not be contaminated by idle thoughts and words.'

They walked away and disappeared.

She was exhilarated by the conversation between the two attendants. Her mind was filled with the form of Sita, who collected the flowers grown by Ahalya and offered them in worship to achieve an early union with her chosen husband. After that Ahalya began to pray to Sri Rama through Sita. At last that moment envisioned by history had come.

He, the handsomest and the most dazzling man stood in front of her, who, by then, had become detached from the emotions of love and hate, to awaken her from her inanimate state.

Even then her only prayer was 'Devi, May your waiting be rewarded soon.'

After giving a new life to Ahalya, Rama appeared in front of Sita.

Ahalya thought, who was more compassionate?

Her detached and saintly husband, who without any compassion, cast her onto bosom of the wide world with the words,' Ahalya, you do not know anything about this illusory world. Do you?'

Or . . .

She had, by then, crossed the boundararies of the forest.

Ahalya turned and looked around in all directions. Had she reached the banks of Tamasa so soon?

How auspicious Tamasa looked! So innocent and pure like the minds of good people. She wanted to stay back and look at the river for some time.

An ominous sound!.

Someone was weeping. She went in search of the person. It was a mendicant woman, clad in the bark of tree. She seemed to be an inmate of Valmiki's hermitage. Ahalya went closer to her and addressed her, gently.

'Oh! Good woman!'

Hearing the voice, she wiped her tears and looked at Ahalya. Ahalya asked, 'In this hermitage, do you have any reason to feel so sad?'

The other woman sobbed, 'How can I tell you? It seems as though the world is coming to an end.'

'What is the matter?' Ahalya stepped closer to her and tried to soothe her.

After a moment or two, the woman said in a hoarse

whisper: 'Sri Rama, the ruler of Ayodhya has forsaken his pregnant wife, Sita.'

'What?' Ahalya gasped with her mouth open. 'Am I hearing the truth?' Her voice was hoarse with helplessness.

'Yes, sister. Some time back, Sage Valmiki, who came to perform the rituals in River Tamasa, found her sitting on the banks, like the very personification of sorrow. The great and generous sage offered his protection to the wife of Sri Rama. I have come in search of the fruits she wanted.'

Before she could complete her sentence, Ahalya's sorrowful, mourning wail pierced the air. 'The fire has abandoned its own flame.'

Nature deserted by its Protector.

This terrible experience . . .

This insult . . .

This hate . . .

The saintly woman, who stood next to Ahalya realised that her voice had grown faint. As she watched, she called out anxiously,

'Sister, respected one.'

There was no reply.

She moved closer to where Ahalya stood and placed her hands on the shoulders of the still figure. She stepped back in fear.

'What! This is just a figure in stone.'

Like a tragic wail, those words echoed and re-echoed on the banks of Tamasa. Hearing the noise, some mendicant women who were bathing in the river came running. They stared without blinking at that beautiful and inanimate figure.

The beauty which dazzled the man whose desire was unabated, even after gazing at it with his thousand eyes.

As they watched, they noticed on its head, the imprint of feet decorated by the shapes of a thunderbolt and a fish.

Later, they looked down at her feet and saw the imprint of Sri Rama's hands on their upper part.

Finally they raised their heads and looked.

Her face had a glow of its own, acquired through long

periods of penance.

They looked at each other and said in the same breath.

'Oh! It is the wife of Gautama.'

The woman sage from Valmiki's hermitage who had become a friend of Sri Rama's wife said in a firm voice.

'Yes, now Ahalya is nothing but a stone.'

Translated by Vasanthi Sankaranarayanan
Published in Malayalam as: Shilarupini

The Cow

M.D. RETNAMMA

When they came back from Divakaran Pillai's house, the father and uncle announced:

'If this works out, it's Kanakam's luck.'

'What enormous wealth! Just the mother and the son. No brothers or sisters. No father. Not even a sister to create trouble and to bicker! And the mother is an invalid.'

Hidden behind the door, Kanakam heard everything. After chewing vigorously, the younger uncle spat into the courtyard and said:

'It is an old *Nalukettu*. Along the edge of the courtyard is a very long cowshed, the like of which there is none in this place. It's so huge, and full of cows. They stand there fat and corpulent, their very sight betokening prosperity. Isn't that so, brother-in-law?'

The father nodded, she could see his face through a chink in the door. What brightness! How pleased he was!

For a while father sat immersed in thought, and then he declared, 'What is the use of a government job? Especially these days? Would such a pittance suffice for anything these days?' He continued after a pause:

'Didn't you, brother-in-law, see the prosperity of that farm? It is about two or three acres, with an abundance of coconut, banana and other types of crops. And all of this is due to the efforts of one person, Divakaran Pillai. Even his milk-business is first-rate.'

Mother sighed in relief on hearing this. She folded her hands and closed her eyes in prayer.

'Everything is her good fortune, Oh! Devi!. . .' At the same time she was anxious.

'But in spite of all this I feel worried. In a house full of cows, there will be a lot of work. Kanakam is not good at anything. She spends all her time playing with the other five children here.'

Father laughed aloud.

'Did you hear this, brother-in-law? This is what is meant by the saying, "the female wit is slow to be lit." Do you think your daughter is going to be married to look after the cows? There are other people for that. Divakaran Pillai himself takes care of all of them. They say he won't let a single person enter the cowshed. He does everything himself, cleaning the shed, milking the cows etc. And what I liked most was his humility. Can one find such a man these days?'

On hearing what father had to say, the second elder sister whispered in Kanakam's ear:

'It is because there is nobody else, that he is always after the cows. Listen Kanakam, it will change when you go there.'

'Go away, Chechi.' Kanakam felt shy.

Divakaran Pillai had asked for nothing, neither gold, nor cash nor a share. He only wanted a nice, modest and quiet girl. He liked her the moment he saw her. Kanakam's father, mother and relatives were relieved. Kanakam was the third of five daughters. The difficulties of the two marriages that had been conducted were not over yet. Two others, younger than Kanakam, although grown-up like her, still remained. But Kanakam was not happy. A government official who went to the office in the morning and returned in the evening, was what she had had in mind. Kanakam had done the pre-degree. During her college days she had seen several such young men whom she thought suitable. She had tried to imagine some of them unexpectedly entering the gates of her house.

'Why don't you say something? Aren't you pleased?' Mother and the elder sisters asked her. She made no reply. The younger sisters said 'Maybe Chechi has some other ideas in her head.'

Mother's voice became harsh. 'What other ideas? No need for them; you won't get a better man. This alliance is more agreeable to me than even those of Saroja or Kamala. Everything is Bhagavathy's mercy.'

Divakaran Pillai tied the *tali* around Kanakam's neck. Sitting beside him in the car, Kanakam did not feel so sad any more. Divakaran Pillai did resemble the figure she had had in mind.

Kanakam saw it just as she placed the first step in her husband's courtyard. It was a long spacious cowshed like a dining hall with cows arrayed like huge elephants. They were watching the wedding procession, their heads held high.

By the evening, the crowds had left. Like a stage after the play, the house lay quiet and vacant. Just her mother-in-law, her husband and herself. And a charcoal-smeared maidservant clad in a skirt, thin as a broomstick.

The mother-in-law went to bed early. Her back ached. She had worked hard for her son's marriage.

Night.

Inside the room, Kanakam was alone. Where was her husband? She had seen him a little while earlier. Her eyes searched for him. The clock on the table in the corner of the room, showed nine. He hasn't even come to eat. Has he gone out somewhere? Isn't tonight the first night? She felt terribly tired and weak. The sadness of having left home and being parted from her family affected her. Restlessness. Her mind was filled with a sense of emptiness.

She stood at the window and unknowingly looked through the darkness outside into the cowshed. There, holding a lantern high in his hand stood Divakaran Pillai! He was scooping up hay with one hand and feeding the cows . . . or perhaps he was massaging them.

She felt sad and angry. 'Should he be doing all this today?'

He saw her standing at the window, and came in immediately. Keeping the lantern in a corner he lowered the wick and said: 'Feeling sleepy, aren't you? But I haven't attended to them today, and they have been waiting for me since the morning. If I hadn't gone now, they would have started mooing. That spotted cow becomes the saddest of them all, if she doesn't see me. Even now when I offered her water she refused to drink it.'

She was not in the least bit interested in his talk, and stood, as though asleep.

'We will sleep after we have eaten. Come.' He walked on, she followed him.

The maidservant was sleeping on the sackcloth in the kitchen. He woke her up.

'Santha! Sleeping at nine! Serve the rice!'

They sat close to each other, but did not exchange a word.

She was not interested in anything. She did not feel hunger either. Inside her mind was a restlessness that seemed just about to break the fence and burst out. A voice whispering:

'This is not what was expected; this is not how it should be.'

She lifted her head and looked. Hay dust and fibres clung to his hair.

He was making rice-balls and gulping them down.

They reached the bedroom again.

'Kanakam, you go to bed. I'll just come. Let me see if they have drunk the water,' he said

Turning the wick of the lamp higher, he went out quickly. She didn't lie down. She stood looking through the window.

She felt angry when she saw her husband going to each cow and whispering something to it, feeding each one separately and affectionately. She felt sad. 'He has greater love for those creatures than for me. He has little interest in me, though I am his bride.'

For the first time she felt enmity towards those dumb creatures, and was overcome by a feeling of revenge. She lay down, restless, and fell asleep at some odd hour.

Sometime deep into night's journey she awoke, shocked.

She had caught the smell of her husband lying close to her in the dark, a smell of hay, cattle-feed and sweat. She turned on her side, away from him. When she got up in the morning and looked through the window, he was there milking the cows, along with his mother who sat close by with milk vessels placed in rows.

She felt angry.

This mother and son have only one thought. Is this their sole occupation? She did not come out of her room, but stayed there obstinately. She hoped that her husband would come looking for her.

After milking the cows he started untying them and moving them to different places.

In frustration, Kanakam came out and began to clean her teeth.

'You've just woken up?' said her mother-in-law. 'See that you bathe and prepare something for Divakaran by the time he comes. Should he still have to eat what the maid-servant cooks?'

Kanakam was angry. But she washed her face without saying anything. Then she asked the maid-servant: 'What do you make usually?'

'Rice-gruel.'

'Oh! That is fine. You can make the same stuff.'

'I made it in the morning,' the maid-servant muttered.

'Very good.'

Kanakam moved into the compound. The hens were ferreting for something at the foot of the banana tree. She wondered whose hens these were.

She walked around the compound. The spotted cow was tied to the coconut tree. It was beautiful to see the black patches on its white skin. Seeing her, the cow mooed.

She felt angry.

She bent down and picked up a stick and, making sure that nobody was around, hit the cow hard with it.

The cow roared in pain.

She hit it again and then muttered with anger. 'You are my

enemy. He has greater love for you than me. I will show you.'

Divakaran Pillai came running on hearing the cries of the cow. She dropped the stick and walked on as if she knew nothing.

'Why did the cow moo, Kanakam?'

Contempt filled her.

What anxiety!

'I don't know.'

Divakaran Pillai started stroking the cow.

'Aren't you having your bath? The water is ready,' the maid-servant said.

'Oh!'

She bathed and put on some fresh clothes. She felt disinclined to wear the bindi and kohl.

The maid-servant asked:

'Aren't you going to line the eyes, or wear kumkum? I have a nice paste with me.' Kanakam noticed then that the girl had been watching her. Wasn't she the guest of this house? Wasn't she the bride? The girl was consumed with curiosity about her.

Kanakam replied, 'I don't like to wear kumkum, I don't line my eyes either.'

Inside, she wished for something else: let my husband ask me, 'Why don't you wear a vermilion mark? Why don't you line the eyes?'

If he asks, I might do so. After all, it is for the husband that the wife wears kumkum and lines her eyes.

A little later.

She saw all the cows of the shed in the courtyard. Her husband was also with them. He smiled and said:

'They like me to take them to the river and bathe them. I take them now and then. It is very sunny today. I shall bring them back after a bath.'

He left with the cows.

Watching them going the mother-in-law explained:

'The cows are his life. Bathing them, feeding them. He thinks of just that while eating or sleeping. He won't hear of appointing someone to look after them. Even for a single night.

He will not sleep in another place. He is more concerned about them than about human beings. Do you know why? His star is the same as that of Gopalakrishnan. His birth corresponds with that of Gopalakrishnan.'

Kanakam felt angry.

She wanted to ask if he had the same nature and habits as Gopalakrishnan and if the Gopikas came anywhere near him.

They came to invite them to dinner : her father, mother, sisters, and brothers-in-law.

A big feast, a treat. Divakaran Pillai displayed his affection generously.

Everyone was satisfied.

But Kanakam looked unhappy.

The sisters noticed it, and said,

'What's happened to you, Kanakam?'

'Nothing is wrong with me.' She did not say anything more, but felt resentful towards them all.

'Perhaps she's feeling homesick after seeing her family. That's why she doesn't say anything,' said her mother-in-law.

Nobody said any more about her unhappiness after that.

Both the cows fell ill at the same time; the cows that were dearest to Divakaran Pillai. One of them beat its legs in pain and rolled about. The other seemed almost dead. Divakaran Pillai was upset. He went out for medicines several times. The mother-in-law sat on the floor of the cowshed and grieved, and was heard saying sorrowfully:

'It is somebody's curse.'

Kanakam was happy. She prayed.

'Wretches! If only they had all died and rotted!'

She did not look at them even once.

At night, Divakaran Pillai slept in the room adjoining the cowshed. Suppose they became worse at night? After all weren't they helpless creatures?

Kanakam gnashed her teeth in the dark, but he could not see the wrath in her eyes.

She lay stretched on the bed. She muttered something, staring at the bunches of paddy sheaves hanging from the ceiling.

All this love for them. A man who does not even have for me a thousandth of the kindness, concern and love he shows to them; it is my misfortune to have become his wife.

She grieved. Wept. Divakaran Pillai did not came to her even after dawn. He was nursing the cows, making medicines and rice gruel for them.

Once, when she looked in that direction through the window, he said loudly,

'Kanakam, Nandini is better. She is drinking water.'

Kanakam turned her head away in disgust.

That night Divakaran Pillai again slept in the dingy room close to the cowshed. When he came in for dinner, he said,

'Kanakam, if you feel scared, call Santha to keep you company. I can't leave them. Suppose something happens at night? I will sleep there.' He walked away.

Kanakam could not help crying.

She felt the sorrow was unbearable. What was this life for? She did not have the position of a four-legged creature . . . becoming a four-legged animal was better than leading a life such as this . . . . She didn't want this life. It was two weeks since she had come here. And still . . .

She rolled about in bed and muttered to herself.

Kanakam did not come out even after the morning was bright. It was well past her usual time for waking up. The mother-in-law waited . . . then got angry.

'Santha, go and look. What a deep slumber . . .'

The maid-servant came back immediately.

'Kanakam Kochamma is not there.'

The mother-in-law was upset. She looked in the bathroom, toilet and the granary.

Now it was late in the morning. Seven, seven-thirty, eight, eight-thirty . . . ten o'clock. Everyone was looking for Kanakam. No one had seen her. Where was she? What had happened? Where had she gone?

Everyone was anxious.

They searched the entire compound. Had she by any chance fallen . . . into the pond or well?

'Oh, no!' Divakaran Pillai dreaded to think of what could have happened.

Shouldn't he inform her people? But what would he say to them? That the wife who was sleeping in his own room was missing? Divakaran Pillai began to sweat.

It was afternoon. Past four o'clock. There was no news of Kanakam. Everyone came to the verandah of the cowshed, disappointed.

Suddenly, Santha cried out:

'Oh! there is Kanakam Kochamma standing inside the cowshed.'

She pointed towards the shed.

Among the herd of cows Kanakam stood, bent over on all fours, chewing the cud, head extended outwards.

Divakaran Pillai called out, his throat choking, 'Kanakam!'

Kanakam groaned loud and long, nodding her head, lovingly and obediently. She put her tongue out and looked at him.

Divakaran Pillai said:

'Santha, bring water. She is thirsty.'

Kanakam went on looking at Divakaran Pillai with gratitude and hope.

He kept a big vessel containing coconut-cake and water in front of her. He stirred it with his hands and pushed it towards her. Kanakam groaned as though brimming with joy. Then, hanging her tongue out, and putting her head into the vessel, she started lapping up the water.

Divakaran Pillai's heart was full. He stroked Kanakam's back with increasing affection. scratched her neck, kissed her hard on the head. Kanakam's eyes began to overflow.

Santha, the maid-servant, stood stunned at the sight.

Translated by Jancy James
Published in Malayalam as: Pasu

In the Temple

RAJALEKSHMY

All that she had striven to build lay shattered around her, in ruins. Pride prevented her from bending and picking up the pieces.

Pride—a meaningless word.

The little mud hut built with clay kneaded with her own hands—the colourful, beautiful hut. In the middle, a grass mat had been spread; the hut, which would have made her feel like the queen of the kingdom of stars. Was it the lack of courage to see it all in a shambles that prevented her from bending? Or was it the fear that she would come across some pieces smeared with her heart's blood?

What was the force that had led her here? Wasn't it only recently that she had felt it would be comforting to sink into the inviting arms of darkness? What was this force?

Born in yuga after yuga, with different bodies, the objects and experiences of all those days must have seeped in and gained a place of permanence in her unconscious. The instincts of earlier births!

This feeling which was considered to be beyond the pale of reason, which had been there from the time of the grandfathers and the great grandfathers, was it mixed with one's blood and lying hidden, beneath the outer layers of material wisdom?

A child runs crying to its mother when it falls and breaks its head. Was she also a child who had rushed, when hurt, to this refuge, considered to be all powerful?

God was embraced by people who were afraid of action! That was what she had said to someone long ago. Did she come here because she lacked the courage to examine the broken pieces of her life, pick out the broken ones and build once again?

Bewildered, she stood at the doors of the *gopuram* of this famous temple.

Were the sorrowful eyes of those who loved her following her?

There was a sea of strange faces behind her.

Were they also afflicted by pain like her? Or were they mere seekers of wealth? Perhaps there were at least one or two seekers of knowledge as well? The Lord stood smiling, His smile heightening the glow of the lamps in the sanctum sanctorum.

She joined her hands in prayer and tried to immerse herself in that smile. What did she expect of Him?

There was only absolute detachment there. The indifferent God of the Kingdom of the Upanishads!

Foolish woman—your heart and your pain, what is so special about them?

Thousands of people, with their innumerable sorrows come to me every day. Are you not also one of them?

I am granite, rock. The smiling idol made of stone!

Are you just stone?

Then—

'Move, come on, pray and move. Do not stand there blocking the sanctum. Yes, move.'

The man wearing a waistband of yellow cloth over his dhoti stood there, between the *mandapam* and the steps to the sanctum. Again it was him.

She moved away from the sanctum.

Every five minutes he came close to the sanctum and he repeated the same words like a machine.

A young man with an unattractive face and a corpulent body. His throat was hoarse with the loud and insistent shouting.

'Either you go there or come this side. If you just stand in front of the sanctum it is difficult for me to manage.' There was a grandmother, holding two children, one by each hand.

'If you don't make room . . .

She realized that he was addressing her.

Through the way opened up by them, a beautiful, young woman also managed to move behind them to the sanctum.

The door of the sanctum was closed.

People thronged both sides of the sanctum. As soon as the door opened, the holy water would be sprinkled, and if a drop fell on one's body, it was indeed a blessing.

One's own body—

Suddenly she heard the sound of drums from somewhere very near her. She moved aside. Along with the sound of the drum came a song, sung in a sweet, lucid voice.

The songs of Jayadeva!

The crowds increased.

'If you recite the name of Hari with love . . .

The indifferent God!

'Hari!', a collective chanting arose.

From the place where she stood, she joined her hands in supplication.

Oh Lord, are You smiling?

'Please move. Move a little. Let me just pray and go . . . what a pity . . . . Please don't touch me and make me impure.'

Those were the Namboodiri women in their wet clothes holding their umbrellas.

'Virtuous mothers! I do not want to touch you. Oh, luckless mothers! You who are forced to restrict your lives within the confines of these palm-leaf umbrellas! I do not want to trouble you.'

As there was no place to move, she pressed herself to the wall and made space. After they left in single file, one behind the other, moving towards the sanctum, the place suddenly became empty. She came out the *nalampalam*.

What a crowd!

She was foolish if she thought she could circle the sanctum without touching anyone. In order to escape from Man, she had come running to this God created by Man.

Oh Lord! Are You laughing?

'Please give me a ticket. One ticket.'

'Ticket?'

A well-rounded, fat boy stood in front of her and begged with hands outstretched.

'I do not have a ticket, child.'

The child went off, murmuring something. He joined a gang of boys, some wearing loincloths, some just a waistcloth. They came in, laughing loudly.

She joined the crowds on the paved circular path around the temple. Was the ceremonial procession with the drum and the lamp coming here as well? She turned and looked.

All she could see was a woman and a man wearing garlands, walking towards her, accompanied by drums and other musical instruments.

'They must be from a rich home. There is music and drums,' an old woman who stood beside her told her friend.

'How much does it cost? Twenty-five?'

'No, For that amount you can get an elephant also,' a third woman said.

Oh Lord! Have they made you too into a trade?

She moved behind the banyan tree.

A middle-aged woman came to her. Her forehead was covered with ashes and sandalwood.

'Please give me that ticket. With it I can get some rice to eat. You will be blessed. I haven't eaten since yesterday.'

'I do not have a ticket.'

'Don't you have a ticket for an offering of rice?'

'No.'

'What about a ticket for an offering of rice pudding?'

'Not even that.'

'Oh!' She went away, disgruntled.

Oh Lord! Was it to encourage beggars that You . . .

'Daughter, have they put the silk cloth?' An old woman who had been lying on a cloth spread near a wall got up and came to her.

'Put on the silk?'

'Have they taken the offerings in a ceremonial procession?'

'I do not know.'

She shook her towel, and putting it on her shoulders, walked off hurreidly.

She moved towards the front door of the temple.

Guarding the door were three or four people with yellow waistbands.

Inside, along with the God, the Brahmins were eating. In front of the door there was a crowd of women, men and children like a swarm of white ants. Everyone was anxious to secure a place in the front.

The door opened, the door through which three people could not enter at the same time.

What a rush!

'Oh! my leg.'

'Trying to be smart? When I am trying to go inside, you keep pushing me out.'

'Don't push.'

Lord! Are You smiling at the anxiety and impatience of these people, Your own children? In Kurukshetra when the brothers quarrelled with each other and killed themselves, were You watching them with the same smile?

Is Your heart made of stone?

The smiling granite statue.

She completed one circle around the temple and came away. In front of the *Gopuram*, the rice-offering was being distributed to the poor. The charity of the haves to the have-nots. The virtue of having distributed rice in the temple surroundings. The old and the feeble!

Long ago, Gautama saw a sick man and corpse.

The server distributed what was available. It was not enough for everyone. Pushing, pulling and beating. Oh Lord!

At last everything was over.

Only three or four people remained. There was a young woman who had fought and got some rice. She took it out of her waist bag and gave it to her blind friend along with some mashed chillies. She assuaged her own hunger by watching him eat it hungrily. A young boy, carrying his tearful sister, comforting her. He had given all the rice he had to her, but she was still hungry.

'Come back, as the rain of compassion.'

Rain of compassion! That can only fall if there are clouds who steal your colour and turn black. Can those white clouds, flitting around like cotton wool, and blinding the eyes with the scorching heat of the sun, do that?

She walked, crossing the last of the lamplit pillars. She came to the marketplace. Where should she go next? Lord! Are You sending back me empty-handed? Earlier, a poor man came to see You with a small bundle of beaten rice, but on seeing You, oh, Beautiful One, he was so taken with You that he forgot to ask for anything. Yet You gave him everything. By the time I reached where I have to reach, will I have gained what I didn't ask for? Will this pain, which has become a part of me, be cured without my knowledge? Will the arid land of my soul be rid of the dry soil and pave the way for life's new green shoots to blossom? Lord!

But then, I am not Your dear friend. You did not forcefully snatch away what I brought You as a present.

To love You . . .

To have faith in You . . .

Oh Lord!

Translated by Vasanthi Sankaranarayanan
Published in Malayalam as: Devalayathil

Incomplete Stops

ASHITA

'Bah! You bitch. Do you think you've been given in marriage here that you can live in this place forever?'

A forceful push sent Annamma reeling to the ground. She found herself kissing mother earth. The door of the cell closed on her with a loud bang. At the jingling of the keys and the sound of the watchman's footsteps, the nearest cell erupted into noise—almost like a mischievous child waiting for a chance to do so. Senseless bursts of laughter, pleas for alms, a cup of tea, a ticket for home, childish complaints, pathetic curses, heartfelt prayers, heart-rending sobs . . .

The watchman's threatening voice rose above the cacophony: 'Shoo! shut up you God-forsaken rascals! Or else I'll . . .' Immediate calm descended at the sound of the swish of the stick. A stray tear fell over a breast in another cell. 'Get up you!' the watchman roared, poking her with his stick. Annamma showly lifted her face—her tears had caked the mud which had dried there. The sun touched her forehead with a compassion that dazzled her eyes—she rose as though uplifted.

'Hey you! Walk!' The watchman's stick swung once on Annamma's back. Annamma walked slowly behind him, dragging her feet. Before her, the spacious hospital compound. Thickly grown plants. At one end of the compound, a banyan tree like a tired and disappointed old man. A sheet of sky, through the leaves, looking compassionately at everything. The huge wall that stands with its head held high against the sky, glass pieces jutting out of it like the little cruel acts of man.

'Oh, Woman! Your misery is over today.' The watchman's words, like tiny bits of broken glass, fell on Annamma, bruising her. 'The committee has met. You will also be discharged today; your misery has at last come to an end but for me there will be relief from here only after I retire.' The watchman carried on, pushing Annamma gently, 'Go! They are waiting.'

They were waiting. The committee members: the superintendent of the hospital, turning the pages of the register, the cat-eyed advocate, always smiling gently, the social worker wearing black spectacles, smiling for no reason at all and with her sari pulled over her head, and the District Collector wearing an air of youthful gravity.

Annamma stood before them with folded hands, puzzled and shamefaced at not hearing the familiar tinkling of the chains.

The advocate's cat eyes watched Annamma, examined her and then the gentle smile returned. Then the superintendent began to turn the pages of her case-history.

'When Annamma, Anna Fernandes, came here she was twenty. It is now ten years since then. At that time she never used to talk to anyone, just laugh without any reason, mutter, cry without any cause, hallucinate . . .' The superintendent declared after a pause, looking at all of them over his spectacles, 'Now everything is cured. Annamma, isn't your trouble gone now?'

'Yes,' Annamma said quietly.

'What does this mean?' the collector asked with the natural curiosity of youth.

'Now, Annamma neither weeps nor laughs,' said the superintendent laughingly, taking off her spectacles and wiping them. 'What is it, Anamma?' 'Oh! . . .' Annamma said, uncertainly. 'Don't you want to go home?' said the social worker with expansive mercy.

'No! No! I don't want to go,' Annamma lost her self-control, and cried out, 'I don't want to go.' A desperate plea, like the last cry of a soul losing itself in the depths of hell.

Like a restless horse, silence raised its hooves threateningly. Suddenly, the superintendent, like an expert horseman who had got hold of the bridle, said harshly:

'Annamma, your illness is fully cured. It is impossible to let you stay here any more. Understand?'

Annamma said in a tired, low voice,

'Yes.'

Interrupting the Collector, who was about to say something, and addressing everyone, the superintendent added in a rather hostile tone:

'All of you here should understand one thing. The Government has made arrangements for only five hundred inmates. Now we have five hundred and thirty persons here. I cannot but discharge thirty of them today.'

'But...' the Collector began to ask something again, stimulated by doubt, characteristic of his youth.

'It is getting late. My clients will be waiting for me,' the advocate reminded him with a quiet smile.

The superintendent returned to the case history.

'Annamma was twenty when she came here. The police who brought her here, found her wandering about, deserted by her husband, who had brought her to this town under the pretext of taking her to Malayattoor church...'

'It is getting late you know . . .' The advocate hinted, looking at his watch.

'Okay! Okay! We will wind up after asking a couple of questions.' The superintendent nodded and looked at the social worker.

She removed her spectacles, and asked Annamma with a mild smile:

'Annamma, what is your name?

Annamma said, seriously: 'Annamma. Annamma, Mannaanam P.O. But pappen alone calls me "Annakutty",'

Annamma added, with a smiling face.

'How sweet!' The social worker was filled with surprise.

'Which is your native place, Annamma?', the Collector asked. The next instant, that question ripped open something in her mind, like a wind blowing hard into a room and pushing all the windows wide open.

Native place! Mannaanam! The hill slopes of Mannaanam on which the wind sleeps with its head resting on its own hands. The lanes in which the warm sun plays about, the maidans, the church . . . . And on a Sunday, the children who followed her shouting . . . . Annamma's eyes brimmed.

'Where is your home' Annamma?' the lady social worker hurriedly repeated the question. Dark clouds of memories crowded into Annamma's wet eyes.

Home! The by-lanes where winds wandered; candles litup in front, Christmas, and Mother waiting with the door ajar; like another melting candle, Mother!

As though even the withered years had suddenly blossomed, Annamma said cheerfully: 'At home, I have mother. My mother!'

'So sweet!' said the social worker affectionately.

'It is getting late for me.' The advocate's smile was now tinged with a sharp impatient edge.

'True. I have to inaugurate a football match in the evening. It is already late.' The Collector had started growing restless for the evening, which promised to be full of glamour and fun.

'Oh Sister!' the superintendent instructed, as he got up, 'Send Annamma off after giving her the bus-charge for the journey to Mannaanam.'

As they were coming out of the hall in a group, the social worker queried: 'Mannaanam? Where is this Mannaanam? Is it a hill station?'

Outside the gates of the hospital, the city received Annamma with an ominous smile. A wind carrying the bustle and smell of the city bypassed Annamma without touching her. Annamma saw a dry leaf flying round and round and at last getting crushed under the sweep of vehicles.

The city was just beginning to immerse itself in the big bustle. A demonstration march came up; slogans were shouted and fists thrown into the air, behind vehicles that moved slowly and blew their horns non-stop. Annamma also joined in at the rear of the procession, enjoying the slogans that rose up with revelry and in a rhythm.

Gradually, the distance between Annamma and the procession that was moving towards the boundaries of the city increased. Annamma was soon left alone in the by-lanes of the evening. But Annamma still kept walking. Her eyes fixed on the hills of Mannaanam, where the wind slept with its head resting on its hands, dreaming of home and a mother, whose sorrowful tears reminded her of monsoon rain.

. . . Annamma walked on . . .

Someone in the shop on the wayside shack coughed once. A whistle from the deserted bus-stop. Someone snapped his fingers at her at the turning of the lane.

But Annamma was walking towards Mannaanam. Still unfamiliar with the freedom that greeted her, with a cheerful and bright mind . . . .

Before long, a policeman at the junction shouted, 'Hey you! Stop there!' Annamma stopped, unconsciously prompted by the memory of the orders in the hospital. 'Up to where is your beat this evening, you bitch?' In the policeman's rage, liquor itself became intoxicated. Annamma, in whose mind her mother's face glowed, gave an extremely charming smile in reply. Then, as the policeman casts sly glances here and there, pats her whole frame mildly with his lathi, shouts in a needlessly loud voice, 'Walk on, you, . . . as Annamma follows him obediently, dragging her feet laboriously, remembering the chains not yet removed from her mind, and as the street lights begin to glow abruptly with a merciless and bawdy smile, my dear reader, how shall I put a full stop to this story?

Translated by Jancy James.
Published in Malayalam as: Apoorva Virnmangal

The Game of Chess

KAMALA DAS

The wrinkles of old age have captured the face of the man I love. When he stands still, or even when he walks, his heavy hands remind me of the lifeless hands of a dancing puppet.

Alone, I sat in the last row of a medium sized theatre thinking of his special features. On the screen a film hero with a broad face was trying to attract the heroine by words and smiles. But I was not able to concentrate on the scene. One part of me—my mature self—kept asking my other, weaker self: why do you love this man who offers you only pain?

I am unable to bear this pain of mine. It is affecting my body too. I lean my head back and close my eyes. My hair brushes against the hard walls. The light emanating from the screen scorches my eyelids. My uneasiness grows. It was as though he had crept inside me; as if his colour, his voice, the smell of his body were mingled with my blood.

A shadow moved in front of me and sat in the next chair. It was a Chinaman. I was temporarily consoled by the nearness of a man.

The name of the film's hero was Presley. He was shaking his hips vigorously and singing. Today, however, his attractive and erotic movements only irritated me. The girls sitting in the rows next to the screen were screaming. I could not understand why they were so happy. It seemed as though I had landed on another planet and was listening to people speaking in an alien language. I had forgotten this language special to youth, I, who was familiar with it only a few months ago.

In getting to know him, did I cast off my youth as well? Who knows? I still laugh. That is, if you can call it laughter, this sound, like the fluttering of a bird's wings, produced by me, in front of others. Every night, before I go to sleep I apply face-cream to ward off pimples. I wear silk saris. But, after performing each of these rituals, I ask myself, 'For whose sake are you doing this? You are the forsaken one.' But, I hadn't expected my fate to be any different. Could I hope for anything else from that happily married man? Yet, on the day when my husband introduced him to me, I was elated in spite of an inner warning that predicted a bad end.

My desire to love grew to become a yawning chasm: early marriage did nothing to help it. Here was a man who was not good looking, but could be trusted and admired. Have I not mentioned earlier, the creases in his face? I found his behaviour falsely modest, but his words were very friendly. That day, what did we talk of? Poetry? I cannot recall.

I just kept listening to his voice. A soft voice, smooth, it rolled like wheels. As I listened to him talking it seemed to me that his mouth was filled with words which kept falling out rapidly.

On that day, darkness swamped the twilight earlier than usual. In his sitting room, the lights were on. He sat against a background of shelves filled with books. I thought of the portraits of writers which appear in magazines. It occurred to me that the room was a stage and the books, the props. He had given to himself the role of an intellectual. I forgave him for the childishness of that setting and the artificiality of his posture. I even went to the extent of loving all that. Had I seen him amidst the middle class glory of potted plants and curios encased in glass cases, I might not have been so attracted to him.

So far, I have not talked of his smile. He has yellow teeth.

One of them is slightly out of line, jutting out. But even this mark of ugliness arouses in me an irrational respect for him.

The Chinaman was now looking at me quite openly. Suddenly I realized that I was crying. I removed my spectacles and covered my face with my hands. I chanted his name soundlessly. Sowmyamurthi, Sowmyamurthi, Sowmyamurthi. Just like a prayer that offers fulfilment through mere repetition. What a name! A name filled with beauty! Is there anything not beautiful about him?

Except my own heart which has now grown old and lifeless.

But this love which I feel towards him, I do not think it is the activity of one organ within me. It is the collective activity of all the parts of my body. Often, my eyes rove his face, seeking to delve into its folds and creases. My cold fingers too have the same intention and they move with a mind of their own. My pathetic hands and legs demand the embrace of those hands and legs, older than them, for their peace of mind. So this love is a joint effort of all these and other parts.

The din in the film increases. A band of musicians wearing black costumes is yelling out a song. The singer stands in front of them in a white outfit. His movements are those of a madman. The audience sits still. The good-looking hero has hypnotized them.

I stood up and wiped my face with a crumpled handkerchief. This film could go on for another half an hour. But I can't bear this loneliness.

'Are you leaving?' the Chinaman, sitting near me, asked. I smiled. Established customs and etiquette may be useful to some mild people who go through their lives without a change of gear. They have no meaning for people like me. 'I came here to forget a man. But I didn't succeed.'

I walked out. As I reached the front of the theatre I saw the street had fallen into a stupor in the morning sun's silvery glow. It was winter. But the day was very hot. Crossing the street to reach my car, I turned and looked back. The Chinaman was standing in front of the theatre, his eyes lustreless from the sun's rays, with the puzzled look of a blind man.

Soon, I started the car. It shuddered once or twice as though my mental turmoil had affected it. I pressed the clutch hard with my left foot. When I think of this meaningless hurry, I feel like laughing.

I drove the car slowly down Strand Road. I saw the ships and the boats, afloat on water. The ships were painted in a cheap, shiny oil paint. They looked like toys. The river had a muddy colour.

I stopped the car, got out and sat on an iron bench, below a tree. I kept telling myself that I would not be able to forget him in this way, for I had sat on this very bench and talked to him. Once he talked of religion. I remember the sun that shone on that day, the wrinkles below his eyes and even the shape of the leaf that fell into my lap. The memory pains me like a sudden slap across my face. He narrated a story to me. The story of a man who bought a mask and kept it in his house. He could not avoid seeing the mask, while he read, ate or slept. Nagged by its ugliness, he smashed it into pieces. But he could not wipe it out of his mind. 'Whatever is on your outer layer will remain inside you also,' Sowmyamurthi said, ending his story. At that moment, I wanted to die. Leaving this mortal body which is like a nest, I would then be free to remain inside his heart. After many years, when he also would be transformed into a soul, both of us would fly back to the old tree and hang from its frame like two bats. As my thoughts took this direction, Sowmyamurthi turned his head to look at me with a smile. A smile, exchanged like a secret gift. My husband, who sat one foot away, did not see the smile.

Now, when I think of that smile I am unable to stem the flow of my tears. What happened to the relationship built during those summer days? I do not know. One day, my husband asked me, 'Is he your teacher?' His voice was filled with pride and joy. For it was he who first introduced me to Sowmyamurthi.

How happy I was during those days! Unbelievably happy! I did not try to analyse our relationship or give it a name. In a way, my love was simple and childlike, like the devotion of tribals. I refrained from asking myself why I loved him. An unsophisticated person does not seek the aid of psychological reasoning or inquiry. His colourful God stays in the temple built for it. What else is needed? In reality, the temple for such a God is not built of mere mud and stone. It is born out of the sense of loss created by the pain of emptiness. In those days, when I walked alone in the dark rooms of my house I sang for sheer joy. Each footstep was part of a dance. I looked in the mirror and smiled. At such times I felt that he was standing behind me. I forgot my loneliness for the first time, after my childhood. I did not have to wear my loneliness like a birthmark and walk around with a heavy heart amidst laughing people.

Some yards away from me a nomadic family from Kathiawar was preparing their food. A young woman walked up and down, stopping to pick up a spoon or a brass plate. The sound of her anklets was soothing. The old men sat in a circle and smoked pipes made of coconut shells. A man with a red turban was leaning on the railings and gazing at me. He looked young. He was also dirty like the others. But I saw in him a certain pride born of youth and an awareness of the importance of one's body. His dark eyes seemed to tell me, 'You may have wealth and beauty. Your body may be sprayed with perfumes. But I know who you are and what you want...' I felt uneasy. I got up and went and stood near that group. A three-year old child with black teeth ran up to me and caught hold of my knees. I lifted her hand and kissed her cheeks. She had the taste of new earth. The woman looked at me and laughed. But I couldn't see any joy in her laughter. Not knowing what else to do I quickly got into the car and left that place.

I had no specific aim. When one road ended, I turned into another. That was all. My eyes were brimming over with tears. The policeman seemed to my eyes to be a misty ghost. I told myself, 'Go back home, Today is Sunday. Return to those rooms where the sunlight does not enter. Go back to those rooms which make you into a sword, resting in its sheath. In

that place, you will not have the cruelty to be yourself. Infatuation is kinder than love. If the feeling that I had for Sowmyamurthi was infatuation and not love, would I have dared to
embrace him on that day? No, I wouldn't. He was not surprised. But he said in a sad voice, 'I am old enough to be your
father, Achala. You know that, don't you?'

In that moment, my soul split into many parts. Each part
voiced its own, different opinion. Only the girl who learnt the
first lessons of love from her grandmother whispered: 'You
are giving trouble to this man. It is better to leave him alone.'
I felt that was the only voice of truth, resurrected from various
voices.

Sowmyamurthi made me sit in a sofa and sat near me. I
thought that he was shivering. In that moment I could have
conquered him. A physical conquest! Such a victory would
have given me only the lowly pleasure of seeing his shame and
guilt. A woman in love is never satisfied if her lover remem-
bers her with only one part of his body. She wishes to grow like
a cancer within him, to fill him with awareness and pain. That
is the special cruelty of love.

He fumbled, faced with my love. He was not prepared to
accept it. The sacrifice of one's body kills only its mortal pride.
But, such a sacrifice destroys the soul's self-respect for ever. I
did not waste my time in consoling myself. In this game,
unknowingly, I had moved my last pawn, an act which could
not be undone. What could I do now?

'Forget, forget,' I went on chanting to myself. But he said,
'You won't be able to forget. Nor can I.'

I felt that those words were benumbing me like a death
sentence. I began to kiss his face thinking, let me win at least
these minor victories. How long he lay like that, I do not
remember. All I know is that he was not eager to wake up from
that sleep or my embrace.

The Bhagavad Gita asks, 'Why does a man commit a sin,
even though he doesn't want to, as though he is being forcibly
made to do so?' My heart was filled with compassion. I had
disturbed his peace of mind, at least temporarily. I ran my

fingers over his face, through his hair. I tried to recall the men I had loved before. Their faces had become blurred like the faces one saw from a speeding train. Each of those relation-ships was like the play rehearsals one had with understudies, in the absence of main actors. This act was devoted just to him. But he was trying to turn and walk away. Even as his lips were subdued by my lips I heard the footsteps of his withdrawal.

I asked him, 'We won't see each other again will we?' Then, unable to bear the truth, I threw my hands around his neck and added hurriedly: 'Promise me. Promise me that we'll meet again.' I remembered another promise. Earlier, I had made my grandmother promise me that she would not die. She was not able to keep that promise. Would this man's words also prove to be false?

'I promise. We'll see each other again,' he assured me. After that, I didn't ever see him again. That was our last meeting.

That night, my husband sat on the bed and began to weep. Silently, without moving any of his face muscles, he shed tears. The quiet dignity of that weeping moved me. I too sat on the bed.

He asked, 'Why did you do that?'

'Do what?'

'You do not love me at all, Achala.'

That evening he had gone to see Sowmyamurthi. In a moment, everything became clear to me. Sowmyamurthi must have told him all that had happened on that day with the cruelty commonly found in people who were anxious to withdraw from anything which had turned out to be like a ritual. I did not feel like offering any excuses. So I said, 'I will not see him again, I promise.'

I decided to keep that promise. I did not want to lessen my burden of guilt through half-truths and palming off some guilt to Sowmyamurthi. He had a position in society, a wife, and children. Nor was he young any more. His shoulders would not be able to bear the burden of guilt. What about me? I was a poor human being who had, for the first time, learnt to love another human being better than herself. I was young. I would take up this burden of guilt like a flag of victory, with courage and pride.

I stopped the car and climbed the steps leading to my house. The door was kept open for me. In the verandah, by the side of a flower vase that held blue flowers that glittered like stars, sat my husband doing nothing. I saw in that face, the haunted look of a caged animal. I did not have even the courage to show compassion.

I took some sleeping pills from the bathroom shelf and sat on the bed. I looked at those pills, hesitatingly, as though they were my enemies. Is this the only way to keep my word?

The God of the Hindus told Arjuna, 'At the time of death if a person remembered another person's form, he would retain the memory of that form and take on that form.' If I died soon after that scene, I would live within him like a sin. I do not want that kind of immortality. I must live within him in beauty, like a smile, or like a shaft of sunlight.

I kept the bottle back on the shelf and and went and stood in front of the mirror. 'Achala, you poor fool,' I told myself, 'After this day your eyes will reflect only your own face. Your ears will hear only your own voice. Let this loneliness be your next love.'

I was amused, for some reason, at the turn that my thoughts had taken. My husband came to the door wondering why I burst into laughter.

I shall not tell him why I laughed.

Translated by Vasanthi Sankaranarayanan
Published in Malayalam as: Chaturangam

Chamundi's Pit

P. VATSALA

Parameswaran married Rukmini to have an assistant in his catering business. His job was to serve rice and curry to the pilgrims who visited the Krishna temple. That was his livelihood, his only mode of earning. Parameswaran took payment in money for the sacred service of giving meals to the people who visited the Krishna temple, situated in the midst of the mountain ranges, for worship, death rites, naming ceremonies and marriages. He earned just enough to make do. There was enough to thatch the roof of his house and buy two sets of clothes to wear. What was the point in wishing for more? Paramaeswaran did not know any other work.

When the road and the bus service were extended to the temple, the number of pilgrims also increased. He needed someone to assist him. A woman seemed to be the ideal solution. She could do the grinding and cooking. She could clear the remains of the food and clean the surroundings: a place where many people came and went. So, he married Rukmini, who was from a distant village, and brought her to his dwelling place. In Parameswaran's eyes, her beauty and education were not important. All that mattered was the great deal of discipline she brought into every aspect of his life. They could now give the pilgrims breakfast as well as lunch. She had the knowhow and the skill to make some simple things for breakfast and dinner.

What then was the hitch in such a carefree life? What did she lack? This was something Parameswaran could never fathom.

The last of the guests finished his dinner and climbed the steps leading to the lodge. Rukmini put out the lamp and closed the door. She sat down in the kitchen and prepared to have her dinner. There was some rice in the basket. She glanced at the wilted plantain leaf and hoped that no one else would come. The hot drinking water had grown cold and was placed on the hearth which still retained some heat. There was no curry left for her. Every day it was the same story. Vegetables were very expensive. She wanted to plant some chillies and brinjals but what with all her daily chores she could never find the time.

She scraped the bottom of the jar of mango pickle and dished out one mango and placed it on her plate. The buttermilk jar was empty, only the smell lingered.

She put back half of the rice she had on her plate into the earthen vessel and moved the basket aside.

She had just begun to eat when, outside, there was the sound of footsteps. She thought that the unlit verandah would make this late guest turn back.

The footsteps stopped near the stairs leading to the verandah.

She peered into the darkness through the open kitchen door.

With her free hand she lifted the kerosene lamp. But the man who had just arrived could see her well. The plate, the edges of her sari and the brass tumbler filled him with some relief. He had missed the bus and had walked a long distance. Tired as he was, all he wanted to do was to sit somewhere for some time. His feet refused to move any further. He was in no condition to climb the several steps leading to the lodge.

His gaze turned to the pot of dried-ginger water in the kitchen.

She couldn't sit quiet any more. Pushing aside her dinner plate and covering it with the plantain leaf, Rukmini picked up the lamp and walked towards the front verandah. Now she could see the guest's star-bright eyes and his thick black beard. His dhoti and long-sleeved jubba were soiled and dirty. The walk through the forest must have done it. He smelt of wild turmeric. He took the bag which hung on his shoulder and kept it on the parapet. He looked longingly at her and then towards the dark kitchen.

Rukmini said, 'Please sit.' She took the rolled grass mat which was kept against the wall and spread it on the floor for him. She lit the lamp which had been put out. In the surrounding darkness the lamp shone with a greater glow. She had filled it to the brim with kerosene, keeping in mind the dark night of the first day of the new moon.

Without uttering a word, she brought the vessel containing dried-ginger water from the kitchen and placed it in front of him.

He drank the water thirstily. The sound was like that of a spring gushing hurriedly to a dry pit. She saw the passion throbbing in the pit of his throat.

She asked, 'have you eaten?' He kept quiet, thinking that it was not right to ask for dinner at such a late hour.

In the distant mountains, a forest fire raged. The smell of burnt raw wood. She thought anxiously, 'this fire will dry up all the springs.'

How would she make rice the next day? Would there be water for the guests to wash their hands? Most of the time they came to wash and cool their feet and faces. They wanted water more than food. Parameswaran used to say that if he sold lime juice instead of rice, he would have become a very rich man. But he believed it was a sin to sell drinking water and make money.

'Can you get a pot of water from somewhere?' he pleaded. She became restless. The washing place in the lodge was dry. Parameswaran had climbed the steps to the lodge and gone to sleep in the first floor verandah, saying that the house was too hot. There was not a drop of water anywhere in the neighbourhood. She understood the agony of the stream, caught between the burning forests, throbbing in pain. After some time even the sound of its cry had diminished, and had lapsed into nothing.

The guest took the *kindi* filled with water, walked to the Kuvalam tree and washed his hands, legs and face under it. She watched, petrified, as he used the remaining water to wash his feet. She was not able to raise her voice in protest. A man tired from walking! Seeing his slim, tall body in the light of the lamp a new image arose before her. His glowing eyes shone like stars in her darkened mind, the stars which appear on the horizon on a night of the new moon. Was it already past midnight?

The prospect of another dawn without water perturbed her. Would another day be born at all?

The leaves had wilted. She served him food in the plate, a pickled mango placed next to the rice. Some of the buttermilk kept aside to set curds for the next day was sprinkled on the rice. This was by no stretch of imagination a meal to be served to a respected guest. She wished she had not asked him about dinner.

Before he began to eat, he looked at Rukmini's face.

'Haven't you eaten?'

Rukmini was flabbergasted. Till that moment no one had ever asked her whether she had eaten. Not even her husband. She kept quiet.

'Please bring another plate. This rice is too much for me.'

Without a word, she washed another plate and brought it to him. Then she withdrew from the front verandah. She was afraid he might demand some curry. Lowering the wick of the lamp, she stood in a corner of the kitchen. It was a dark corner from where neither of them could see each other.

He ate silently. There was not even a pappad to fry. She was unhappy. Usually she kept a stock of salted and dried beans and bitter gourd, and pappads made of jackfruit for serving her special guests. She had even planted many vegetables near the kitchen courtyard for this purpose. The summer licked off everything. When the mountains burnt and the forest streams died with their throats parched, she was surrounded by a veritable desert. The rain seemed to be far away, somewhere beyond the mountains. There was not even a hint of a slight breeze that could grasp the rain clouds by the hand and lead them here.

She heard the guest get up after his meal.

She shivered. Where would she get him water to wash his hands?

The pots, pans and vessels in the kitchen were all empty and upturned. There was some boiled water kept aside for drinking. She poured a glass and brought it to him.

As he washed his hands, the guest looked at her face sideways.

She said softly: 'The water is finished.'

He gave her an astonished look.

'A scarcity of water in this place?' But then he sighed, looking at the garlands of red fire on the horizon.

Later, she decided not to have supper.

She put the pots and pans in order. As she was closing the door, the guest said, heaving his bag onto his shoulders, 'I am going to the lodge to sleep. Where can I go to bathe in the morning?'

In the dark, she pointed to the distant bathing ghat.

'You have to walk quite far. There is water only in the Chamundi pit. It is actually a deep pond.'

As he climbed the stone steps and disappeared into the courtyard of the temple, Rukmini stared at the steep walls that loomed in front of her like Fate. Those walls carved out from rock; below, a piece of raised ground like a prison. No one, not even a stray breeze had paused to look at her little thatched hut.

It was past midnight. When the hearth cooled, perhaps her husband would come down the steps of the lodge. Perhaps he wouldn't.

Closing the doors from the outside, she spread a mat in the

front verandah. The mat smelt of wild turmeric, from the unknown guest.

She tossed and turned, not able to sleep. Her young son, who woke up from his sleep came to her, mumbling something. He stretched out beside her. She knew that he was perspiring. She picked up the arecanut-spathe fan and fanned him to sleep.

Somewhere, far away, a barren thunder trembled. The leaves in the higher branches of the trees in the courtyard rustled. Then she slept. The noise of a footfall woke her.

It was not yet dawn. High above, one or two birds chirped. She opened and closed her eyes, and then began to search for something near her.

A torch shone. 'What have you lost?' said a voice from the courtyard. In the light which tore the heart of darkness, she turned her gaze to the mat once again.

Nothing. Just emptiness. Bitterly, she remembered that her son was just a dream. A wasted shoot growing on a branch stuck in dry soil. Even before it could see the daylight, it had withered away.

She tried to forget her dream and smile.

The guest murmured, 'I am going in search of a drop of cool water.' He sought her eyes questioningly.

She folded the mat and joined him.

Translated by Vasanthi Sankaranarayanan
Published in Malayalam as: Chamundi Kuzhi

The Guest Who Came in a Palanquin

P.R. SHYAMALA

The *Thampuratti* sat in a velvet-cushioned chair, in front of a large mirror with a carved frame. Tathi looked at the lady's glorious face reflected in the mirror, as she ran her fingers through the proud woman's long, wavy tresses, taking out the knots to make them attractive.

She was the lady's faithful handmaid. She could even be called her dearest companion.

Tathi looked at her lady's blue silk blouse embroidered with golden flowers and thought how well it suited her complexion.

Entrusted to look after the lady's personal comforts, she moved very closely with her. She routinely assisted in the lady's bath and worship, handing over her clothes, helping her to get dressed and making the bed. So she had many opportunities to get to know the lady intimately.

The lady had not told her where she was going on that day. Nor did Tathi have the courage to ask. All of a sudden, the lady declared: 'After laying out the bed, you can go down. Today, I will be going to the Manchoor palace.'

Tathi's face cleared. Assuming a coy expression, she straightened the lower edge of the gold-bordered cloth covering her lady's breasts and said: 'I knew it when I saw you preparing so meticulously for your bath.'

'Away with you, you wicked girl!'

Lady Ratnamayi's nosering and the vermilion mark on her forehead enhanced her beauty. She was going to Manchoor Palace to meet her husband, who would be waiting for her eagerly, counting the seconds. A person with her lady's temperament deserved to be told by her husband, 'If you wish to see me, you will have to come to me, wherever I am.' But he never uttered these words.

Tathi continued arranging the bed and the lady went downstairs.

Tathi glanced through the window. The palanquin and the palanquin-bearers were there, waiting. She finished her work and ran down. The quick patter of her steps made no sound on the carpeted floor.

As the lady bent a little to enter the palanquin, Tathi saw a rose adorning her hair, fastened at one end. She must have plucked it herself from the rose bush in the front courtyard.

Four men lifted the palanquin onto their shoulders. Other attendants followed.

The journey to Manchoor Palace! The journey to her bridal chamber!

Why were *Thampuran* Udayavarman and *Thampuratti* Ratnamayi staying in two different places? Hadn't they cleared up the misunderstanding between them? It was difficult to decide which of them was more stubborn. But because of this, for a long time they had been living separately. Anyway, whatever the reason for her lady's stubbornness, wasn't she a woman after all?

No one knew exactly why, a long time back, those two had quarrelled. Only the faithful attendant Kannan had been heard to say. 'I know the reason'. Kannan's father too had been an attendant in the palace. Tathi, who knew her lady intimately, was naturally anxious to know the reason for the misunderstanding.

In fact, Kannan had become friendly with her by saying he could tell her why they'd quarrelled. So far, he had not actually told her anything. Once he had hinted that there was no serious dissension between the *Thampuran* and the lady, and it was just a playful, amorous quarrel. But even then, he did not reveal any details.

The lady lived in dignity, as befitted her position and status. She fiercely opposed the world's inequities and injustices. But even as she fought against those evils, she bore in her heart the sweet pain of separation.

Her intense quest to find solutions to the people's problems made her keep her own dreams locked up in an iron chest.

Now, when she made these occasional trips to meet her beloved, her well-wishers felt happy for her.

Her mind full of the fond good-byes uttered by her lady, Tathi crossed the gatehouse to reach the southern courtyard. As she came near the jasmine bushes two strong hands shot out and caught hold of her. Strong arms tightened around her. Startled, she looked up and saw Kannan's handsome face.

'Leave me, please.'

'Why, are you frightened? Why don't you stop for a moment and enjoy yourself?'

'Oh no, someone will see.'

Then, Kannan whispered in her ear. 'Didn't you see your lady going? Does she tremble and flap her wings like you? You ask her.'

'But isn't he the lady's lawful husband?'

'You will also become my wife.'

For quite a few days Kannan's love had put her in a dilemma—a love too sour to swallow but too sweet to spit out.

Could she trust Kannan?

They had been seeing each other behind the pillars, in front of the gatehouse. But Tathi never crossed the limits of propriety. If anything untoward happened, her mother would kill her or commit suicide. She lived in the village beyond the fields, the mountains, and the thickets of grass, praying for her daughter's well-being.

Once a year, her mother visited her—when the mangoes ripened on the tree that stood on the southern side of her small village hut. Filling the mangoes in a basket she had woven herself, her mother would bring them from the village to present them to her lady.

'Old mother of Tathi! Do not feel worried about Tathi. No danger shall befall her.'

In the moonlight when she gazed at Kannan's handsome face, she was reminded of her lady's words to her mother.

'No danger shall befall her.'

Who had uttered these words? None other than Lady Ratnamayi, the Preserver of Dharma, who could sense from afar the injustices and dangers that pervaded the country and provide remedies for them.

The lady would definitely protect her from all dangers.

Tathi could not contain her impish laughter. Was Kannan who invited her, on the days when the lady visited Manchoor Palace, to come to the platform near the pond outside the gatehouse, a danger to her? Even if he was, wasn't her lady there to protect her?

Kannan brushed back her unruly hair and planted a kiss on her forehead. The lady's faithful attendant! At a command from the lady, Kannan was prepared to cut off anyone's head and make a present of it to her. He was ready to protect her from anyone, even to sacrifice his own life.

If the lady requested, Kannan would protect Tathi too. It was this firm belief which finally emboldened Tathi to cross the prohibited boundaries. After all, it was the lady's goodwill towards them that had served as a link between them.

They sat in the dark and exchanged stories. The jasmine creepers were laden with unplucked flowers. Their fragrance reminded them of the heavens above.

At last, Kannan held her by the shoulders and gave her a playful shove. 'Now you must go. It is getting late.' She lost her balance for a moment and hit against the parapet wall.

With a pout she exclaimed, 'Oh! my poor back!' Kannan

burst out laughing.

The next day, when she woke up and went to bathe in the pond, three or four withered jasmine blooms, stuck inside her blouse, fell into the water.

She sat on the steps of the pond and took some water in the palm of her hand. The jasmine blooms floated in the water. That was the day of the festival of the temple. The lady arrived at the temple with full ceremony. The drumming for the *Sivabali* could be heard from a distance.

Tathi sat in a corner of the inner verandah nodding her head sleepily. Someone came and woke her.

'Tathi, the lady wants you.'

Tathi sprang up, washed her face, and wiped it with a cloth. Then she went up the carpeted stairs.

The lady was sitting on her bed. She took the jasmine garland from her hair and put it on the bed.

'Tathi.'

'Your honour!'

Tathi stood there, ready to carry out her lady's commands. 'Why are you looking a bit tired?'

Tathi went pale.

'I slept very little. Forgive me. Please do not be angry with me.'

'Even during the day you look tired?'

Tathi stood there and trembled.

'I do not feel exhausted.'

'If you are not feeling well, go home for a few days.'

'I am not unwell.'

Tathi thought for a while. She could see no visible change in her lady's expression. She went down the stairs, clutching the banisters as she felt extremely tired.

How could she tell her lady? Maybe she should go and see the lady along with Kannan. Let Kannan tell the story. She would just stand there, with her head bowed.

Or should she tell the lady after the marriage ceremony? That would be impertinence on her part, as both of them were the lady's faithful attendants. One thing was clear to her. She would get married only with the lady's blessings and best wishes. That was certain. As she lay down to sleep, the memory of the erotic postures depicted in the sculptures on the ceilings stirred new desires in her heart. Her thoughts shifted to Kannan and the embracing figures sculpted on the pillars became sweet remembrances.

Still, she shouldn't have done it!

A pregnant bride!

What could she do? It just happened. The white lilies in the pond would bear witness to the event. The unplucked jasmine flowers left on the creepers, the stone-lamps in the gatehouses with their wicks burnt out and the moonlight which transformed the surroundings of the palace into a milky sea, were all witnesses.

Good or bad, right or wrong, she would never be able to erase from her mind, the haunting nights when they whispered sweet nothings to each other.

She kept her face close to Kannan's chest, wept and implored him: 'Please do not delay. . . I want not only life but self-respect.'

Kannan began to laugh.

'Stupid girl, why are you crying?'

'Tell me, when is our wedding? It should be soon. Then we would have to tell the lady only about the wedding.' Kannan stroked her back consolingly

'Why are you so worried? Don't we have enough time for that?'

Tathi was relieved. She went back and slept peacefully.

Several times, Kannan saw the lady to discuss matters of importance and he travelled to many neighbouring countries as the lady's messenger. Tathi shuddered and fear clutched at her heart with the growing movements within her womb.

She stood behind the stone on which a love-poem was inscribed and reminded Kannan:

'The child inside my womb.'

'Don't worry, Tathi, let it grow. Don't you believe that I will give you the bridal sari?'

The working season came. It was very difficult for her to even see Kannan. Lady Ratnamayi went to the Manchoor Palace two or three times. In the palace hall, dance performances and music concerts were held.

Tathi continued to attend on her lady. When she had a ceremonial bath, Tathi handed her garments to her. She arranged the bed and assembled the articles required for the puja.

Even though the lady was older than Tathi, she joked with her, forgetting the difference in age and position. At such times, the lady never treated Tathi as a mere servant.

It was on such occasions, when the lady stretched herself on the beautiful mattress on the ornamental cot, entertaining idle thoughts, that Tathi felt like telling her about Kannan. But she could never muster up enough courage.

The months went by. Once she waylaid Kannan deliberately in front of the stone lamp. Tearfully she asked him:

'Don't you see my swelling stomach?'

'Seeing your stomach, no one can guess that you are pregnant.'

'Oh! Please stop this painful humour of yours. When are you going to marry me?' Her voice faltered.

Kannan burst into laughter. Tathi was startled.

'My dear Tathi, I am alive, am I not?'

'That won't do.'

Kannan's face changed. In a grave tone he declared, 'Why don't you leave me alone and allow me to carry out the lady's orders in peace? What a nuisance!'

Tathi bowed her head in silence.

Kannan rushed out, beyond the walls of the palace. He mounted a black horse and galloped away.

She heard the rhythmic clatter of hooves. As the sound faded into the distance she looked around, realising her plight. She was alone, without any help, with no one to support her. She broke into a run, as though she finally understood Kannan's deceit. Crossing the verandah with stone pillars, walking beneath the kerosene lamps, she stepped onto the soft,

carpeted floor. She began to run again. She mounted the stairs
and reached the inner verandah, when she heard the sound of
the tanpura from the lady's room. She realised then that she
did not have to lean against the wall for support or break into
tears while she recited her story, because there was a lady who
wielded power and could find solutions to problems. Still, she
cried as though her heart would break.

The sound of the tanpura stopped. Tathi closed her eyes.
The lady asked:

'Tathi what is wrong?'

She fell at the lady's petal-soft feet.

'Get up.'

She did not get up.

'I say, get up.'

Hearing the command she got up.

'Tell me, what is the matter?'

She related her story in a broken voice.

'Impertinent rascal!'

'Please forgive me.'

The lady walked into her room with a serious expression
on her face. Going near the bed, and pressing her fingers on the
tanpura she said:

'I will definitely speak to Kannan. How can I allow him to
do you this injustice?'

Tathi opened her eyes wide in surprise. Was she hearing
correctly? Why, the lady had never once been unjust. She had
always recognised the truth. So she would protect her also.
The lady had in the past ruthlessly suppressed injustice. The
hands of those who harmed the people had been cut off. Let
Kannan learn a lesson! He was familiar with the tripod and
scaffold. Let him realise that he couldn't go very far, mounted
on that black horse!

Tathi bathed, changed her clothes and went about her
routine jobs, her mind at peace. She would be pleased to see
Kannan cringing like a thief before the lady. As she was
stringing the jasmine flowers into a garland for the puja room,
the lady came out.

Tathi go up.

'Kannan has come back. I shall speak to him.' For her, those were moments of hope, moments when proceedings were being initiated against injustice and high-handedness.

Days passed with ease, like flowers shedding their petals. Lady Ratnamayi went to Manchoor Palace. She concluded a treaty with a neighbouring country. She devised new plans for the welfare and prosperity of her people.

Discussions were held with all the top-ranking officials. The Royal Durbar Hall was always crowded. Public wells, public lodges—the emphasis was on providing facilities for the common people. Little doves flew up in the air, with messages of peace.

Tathi had a tough time concealing her enlarged stomach. She did not have the courage to ask her mistress:

'Lady, what did Kannan say?'

But one day the lady herself called her and told her, 'You must see Kannan. I have explained matters to him. Soon he will marry you.'

A breeze laden with the fragrance of roses shook the lady's curls and lifted the dark clouds in Tathi's mind.

She waited beside the pillar which had the engraving of an embrace. When Kannan came that way, she called out to him. She couldn't bring herself to say anything so she wept.

'Why are you groaning, Tathi?'

'Oh God! How can I describe to you the fire in my heart?'

'Wouldn't I have quenched it? Why did you have to tell the Lady?'

'Won't you protect my honour? The months are flying . . .'

'So what? Do you think I won't marry you?' Kannan consoled her.

She realised that Kannan's love for her was diminishing and gradually shrivelling up.

Even if he married her it would be only out of fear. Still, it would give her a chance to regain her honour.

Kannan was preparing to go to some distant place at the lady's behest.

'When will you be back?'

'After four or five days.'

She was relieved. That day, as the lady bathed, she expressed her sympathy for Tathi's physical discomfort.

'Tathi from now on, you don't have to work. Let Kunhikutty come and do it. You can go to your home. I have told Kannan everything.

'Kannan' . . . Tathi began hesitantly.

'Don't you have faith in my words?'

'I will go away. By now, most of the people here know of my condition. It is only my mother . . .'

'I shall send Kesu and Kunhikutty along with you. They will explain everything to your mother.'

'Yes, Your Honour.'

'Farewell! You will do well. You acted thoughtlessly and made a mistake but you've had to suffer a great deal as a result of it. Basically you are not a bad person so everything will turn out all right.'

Tathi left the palace, and its precincts knowing that her future hinged on the lady's words. She walked along the fields, crossed the hills and forests and reached the courtyard of that small house with the branches of a sweet mango brushing against its roof.

Her mother was startled to see her. But when Kesu and Kunhikutty explained everything she was relieved.

Tathi's life became one of waiting. The mornings saw her wake up, waiting for Kannan, the queen's attendant, who rode a black steed and galloped through the fields and valleys. Her twilights saw her going to sleep, still waiting for him. She hoped that her wedding would take place before she delivered the child. The memory of Lady Ratnamayi, the Preserver of Dharma who found remedies to a hundred instances of injustice, was engraved in her heart.

Every day she made it a point to climb the hill behind her house to keep watch. To see whether Kannan was coming on a black horse. But she never saw that figure, not even as a black dot in the distance.

One day a palanquin carried by men was seen in the valley. The pregnant woman leaned against a tree and watched its progress intently. As it came nearer, it seemed to grow in size.

Below, on the road in front of her house, the palanquin was set down.

A beautiful woman of noble bearing stepped out of the palanquin. She climbed the steps leading to the house, and reached the spot under the tree, before the pregnant woman.

'You won't give birth to a child, without having a husband. I have taken care of that situation.'

The young woman was visibly annoyed at these words.

'I am not going to deliver a baby without having a husband. Look!'

She pointed to a youth who sat in the courtyard weaving cane baskets.

The proud lady stood there perplexed.

At that moment, an old woman came out of the house.

'My lady, bear with that girl and forgive her.'

Then she signalled the girl to go inside.

The girl did as she was told.

'My lady! Why have you come to my humble hut?'

'To see Tathi. To make Kannan give her the bridal garments.'

The old woman laughed ruefully and said:

'Tathi does not need the bridal garments any more. She waited to deliver her child, not wanting to take its life. Then she jumped into the pond below and killed herself.'

'I thought I saw Tathi just now.'

'That is not Tathi but her daughter Chinnakutty. This is her lawfully wedded partner. She is in her eighth month.'

Lady Ratnamayi hung her head and returned down the steps. After she stepped inside the palanquin four men lifted it onto their shoulders.

The palanquin then moved along the banks of the fields, through the path in between the cluster of rocks to the road covered in red soil.

The pregnant woman watched from the shade of the tree.

The palanquin eventually became a black dot in the distance.

'Who was that, Grandmother?'

'The *Thampuratti.*'

Was the pregnant woman satisfied? She leaned forward and looked.

She could not see the palanquin any more.

Translated by Vasanthi Sankaranarayanan
Published in Malayalam as: Manchalil Vanna Atithi

The Third Night

NALINI BAKEL

From the moment I got to know Devanand I knew, at least in my subconscious, that I was destined to venture out on a trip like this. I felt a strange restlessness whenever I thought of the task of winning Devanand over at the cost of my loved ones. I would think of the inevitability of this happening, and would, at moments, even feel upset about it. But I would justify my actions by reminding myself that life was full of adventure and one had to live dangerously.

Yet I was gripped by a nameless anxiety when I started on this journey one evening. It was only the thought of my mother—who would probably have supported me—that kept me going, and I hoped that she might even forgive me one day. Busy with my thoughts I sat, like the others, looking out.

But by now, the beginning of the third night and at this time of evening, I was less anxious than I had been before. The cool mountain breeze was soothing and lulled most of us into a delicious sleep as the bus climbed up the pass. All of us, fellow travellers, were quite exhausted by the long journey. I slept, supporting myself on the iron bars, and consoled myself with the thought that this was the third night and the journey would be over, and that the dreams that had so far remained suspended in a state of tense fearfulness would soon come true. I think I must have fallen into a deep sleep as the shores of tragedy and despair seemed to have receded.

So what if I was alone?

I had no precious ornaments on my neck and hands. I had only one or two dresses in the bag. So I came to the conclusion right at the beginning, that there was nothing to fear. And the fellow travellers, who had earlier been strangers, had by now become familiar.

The bus was really flying. I should admit though that this unusual speed did not upset me. In fact, I was lulled into thinking that I had become a real angel like the ones I used to be transformed into in my imagination, as the waves washed away Devanand's name which I would draw in the damp sand on gloomy evenings, waiting to fly to the unknown town where he worked. I was in a sort of trance, believing that the bus was plying, without touching the ground, to an unknown golden destination, my white sari flapping like a bird's wings.

My body had begun to ache. Although I wanted to move my numb knees, stretch my limbs and walk about a little, I decided not to, knowing that it would disturb my sleeping fellow travellers. Also, I was a little unnerved by a man who kept staring at me. In that benumbed state, I might have slept again but I woke up shocked, at hearing a loud cry, just at that moment when I was dreaming of Devanand's pleasant face.

When the initial shock was over, I realised it was like a girl's cry. Outside, darkness, shadows and moonlight were performing a ritual dance. There were small valleys on either side of the mountain pass and deserted thick, small forests dotted about.

As the bus headed forward, the cry continued to be heard. I was amazed. That cry was initially intermittent, now clear and later faint, as though the bus was going round in a circle. At last it ceased, breaking down as a pathetic wail, somewhere in the dark outside.

A terrible fear engulfed me. As the bus was climbing up the pass, bending and twisting through the same road it suddenly shook as though caught in a difficult predicament.

Many of those who had woken up, were trembling with

fear. They lay back with their eyes shut, as though they were trying to withdraw inwards and escape into sleep. I was afraid of shutting my eyes and looked repeatedly at each fellow-traveller, my heart beating fast. The man who sat next to me woke up staring, but reclined against me, after making sure that I was not quite asleep yet.

I shuddered in spite of myself and looked around. The man in the front seat who was idly looking at me from the very start, seemed to have observed my expression.

To my great amazement, he shouted:

'There's nothing to fear. This is usual.' Hearing those words of consolation the young man sitting next to me opened his eyes. He jumped up, from his leaning position and said:

'Stop the bus!'

The driver was driving, detached, unmindful of anything. His heavy head which lay loosely on his flat and flabby neck swayed to and fro to the rhythm of the bus, as if in a cosy drowsiness. He sat unmoved, with his half shut, blood-red eyes and hanging head, like a person used to seeing all this.

The man beside me would have shouted at the sight of the driver's indifference. But the traveller in the front seat said once again.

'Don't stop the bus. This is something usual.'

The other one said, astonished.

'What! What silly things are you saying?'

The traveller added in the same old careless manner: 'They are cutting that girl up and killing her. When the earlier bus stopped, they must have forcibly taken the girls off. If this bus also stops . . .'

He looked at my face.

As I shivered and was visibly subdued, I looked at the man who seemed willing to help me, craving for pity.

But the argument had become so intense that neither of them was willing to give in.

I wanted to cry as I realised that the attention of all the passengers in the bus was on me. In a flash I saw my helplessness. Devanand had once written to me that the womb was a punishment too—the last year that had passed by in shame, because of the slogans I had raised about women's empancipation . . . my job which I lost because of my article on male domination!

'My God!'

I was a fool!

I had set off for Devanand dreaming of that equality, stamping cruelly on the love and attachment of those that I needed . . . .

At the end of the journey—when the dreams were within reach—unexpectedly, when I realised that tragedy was just before me, and that there was no escape, I said pathetically:

'Oh, Please don't stop the bus.' My plea melted into waves in the mountain breeze.

As everyone watched, and in a move for which I was least prepared, the passenger who had demanded the bus be stopped, jumped up. Before the other person could prevent him, he clutched at the driver's neck.

The driver must have lost control in that violent fight. The bus was hurtling downwards. A loud cry from the crowd. . .

Now it is all silent. Desert all around. And peace too.

The third night was silently advancing into the dawn. A blood red glow in the East.

I could feel an intense pain as I recovered consciousness. There was a dampness where I put my hand. It could be blood.

That morning brought me consciousness of Devanand. Devanand who was waiting for me at the bus stand in the town. Poor Devanand!

For a moment the memory of Devanand did not allow my consciousness to leave my frame. But in the next moment, the last remnant of that consciousness in the bus, parted with my being.

As the waves washed away Devanand's name from the damp sand, I became an angel. But the journey was towards a place where there was no Devanand.

Translated by Jancy James.
Published in Malayalam as: Munnam Ravu

The Sword of the Princess

MANASI

As the bud-like flame of the match-stick glowed so close to me that I could touch it, I thought only of one thing: why not set fire to the edge of my dress with it? My clothes would then slowly catch fire evoking the beauty of a blossoming bud. Held within the attractive flames, I will become beautiful like the goddess Saraswathy rising up from the centre of the lotus as shown on the calendar hanging on the wall at home. I might even become unconscious in the brilliance and heat of the glowing flames. Then they would burn with a rhythm. Almost calm and quiet. Or perhaps, I might then evoke memories of a river, full, that proudly flows along its banks. The beauty and motion of the flames always reminds me of waves.

But all this would happen only if I could attain the same dignity and peace as the flames that rise around me. This is possible for a human being. I might, despite my resolve, cry out aloud. When my husband wakes up, he will stare at me standing within the flames. He might then search for some water and a woollen blanket, mentally cursing my indifference. I think I would be happy at his embarrassment. It has become a necessity for me to win. I have almost reached the limits of my patience, after continuous surrender. I have to win a victory over the dreams which, for a long time now, constantly frighten and amaze me, make me helpless, and also over my egotistic intellect that audaciously seeks the reason for everything—why I eat, why I love, why I am what I am. I have often felt that I will somehow succeed in this attempt when I stand at the centre of the flames; when they remain, opposing my will and dreams, at a point from which they can no longer touch me, wearing on their faces an expression of having been deceived, just as does my husband. The sorrow over the prey that escaped from the mouth. That is what will make me feel excessively happy. They wouldn't enter this glowing heat on their own, because they'd be afraid to burn their fingers. Thus, when I stand happily inaccessible to all of them, I might shout loudly: 'I love you all! Everyone who loves fire and its heat cannot but love human beings.' I have always wished to say this, standing beyond the sterile, inadequate boundaries set by rational thinking.

The match-stick had died out. The cold water on the stove and my crumpled sari are as before. Just the burnt out match-stick lay in bits on the cooking slab. Slowly, as I kept the water to boil, everything began to look incredible and strange to me. I had lain down alone in the darkness last night in a corner of the long corridor. That corridor, surrounded by thick stone walls, had no doors leading towards the outside. My mind, a chip from those well-cut and polished walls, could be seen through my skin, like a piece of granite lying under clear water. My mind was infinitely calm, like a pond without waves, its surface frozen. I rolled several times from one end of the corridor to the other, on its shining floor, holding that mind within me. How many times! At last, I began to cry loudly. But my voice did not sound like that of a human being. I quelled that sound, which was too frightening and piercing to have come from my throat. I wished to cry aloud but I kept quiet, not even opening my mouth, being frightened of my voice. That's why I started rolling over again and again. Just then I noticed a small piece of iron on the floor over which I had rolled about so many times. I tried to use it, to cut the walls that stood cold-faced around me. I realised that just next to those walls lay my child, and the world, and also dishes made with plenty of chillies and salt. I scratched the stone walls again and again with that rusty iron piece. Making passages into that palace of peaceful, trouble-free death, and going back into my past life and going into the midst of my friends, I longed to cry, just once, like a human being. The iron piece was reduced to half, because of the scraping. I began to strike my head against that stone. It was surprising; it did not give me any pain. But I did wake up sometime around then. It was unusually late. I felt inexpressibly tired and cheerless. All I felt like doing, was to get up slowly and, without even combing my hair, to walk about in the coolness of the dawn outside. I know all that is impossible when there are a hundred and one things to do at home. But I just lay down there, not bothering to do anything.

'Aren't you getting up today? asked the husband.

'Don't feel like getting up,' I replied.

'What fatigue!'

'What causes such fatigue?' the husband asked. 'Fatigue! Even after a sound sleep and after snoring the whole night?'

'I am getting up,' I said, rising. 'I had a strange dream yesterday.'

'Oh?' he queried. 'You are not the only one: everybody has dreams. So what?'

I shook myself. Every inch of my body was steeped in fatigue even as I walked into the kitchen after washing my face, carelessly leaving my sari in an untidy and crumpled heap. I think I had rolled non-stop along that corridor for a long time. As the memory of that doorless corridor flashed, I stopped abruptly. I slowly stretched my fingers and examined them anxiously, much as one looks around after reaching home on dark nights, in case a thief is hiding behind the open door—even though you know that is foolishness. My beautiful fingers were still clean, long and rosy.

As soon as I reached the kitchen, I opened the windows noisily as though wreaking vengeance on someone. Wind suddenly rushed inside, like an enemy. How much better even the presence of the enemy feels, than being left alone! I sat down on the stool nearby, terribly exhausted as well as relieved. I think it was while sitting there like that that I fell asleep.

I woke up hearing the husband brushing his teeth. His face was swollen with anger. I pretended not to have seen it. What else must I pretend not to have seen? My own dreams, my husband's angry face, the face of the beggar boy for whom I throw down chappatis from the balcony, fading into the face of my darling son, and the dirty flies that fly around the head and body of my poverty-stricken maid-servant who collects the leftovers from the plates dumped for cleaning and stuffs them into dirty aluminium vessels to feed her children.

The husband made tea. The tea leaves, and the match-sticks I had broken lay untouched on the cooking slab. I put the milk to boil and, as I washed my face, splashing plenty of water, I began to think, without any apparent reason, about the beggar boy who resembled my son. I should tell him to come here one day, when I am alone, with nobody around, I thought. And then I would take him to the bathroom, bathe him, scrubbing him vigorously with soap, dress him up in new clothes, give him lots of food, and put him to sleep on my lap. And then? Let us not think of that, I said to myself. What lie would I tell the *gurkha* who guards the gate, in order to let him in? The *gurkha* would stare at me contemptuously. Even if I were to ignore him and order him to send the boy into the house, with all the dignity given me by the ornaments adorning my body and the costly sari draping it, he might oblige, but he could make a public scandal. Then the decent inhabitants of the building in which I live, might lament over my wilfulness, and unbecoming conduct or misdeeds. That is what always happens, when the measuring-rods for gauging one's decency are held by other people. And my husband will come to know of it, eventually. The milk I had kept on the fire boiled over and streamed down as I was washing my face thinking about all these things. Staring at it for a while, I put off the stove. My excessive langour made my husband angry. He stood unmoved, staring at me, holding the bath-oil in his palm.

I watched the drops of oil dripping through his fingers and then, as though nothing had happened I said, 'Let me go out for a while. I think I am very tired.'

My husband stood in the same position as before, not moving his hand even once. But as I walked past him he caught hold of me and stopped me forcibly. 'Leave me,' I said. 'I shall be back soon.'

But my husband's grip was firm and hurtful. His face became dark with anger and looked as though some charcoal was smeared on it. Suddenly, without any reason, I started thinking about that dark, doorless corridor along which I rolled so many times. It was at that moment—that is what I realised when I thought about it later—that I was overcome by anger. I felt that I could release myself from my husband's grip with a slight jerk of my arm and that he was being as silly as a child. Contempt, anger, intense derision and blind force spluttered from within my mind like the embers scattered from a burning pyre. 'Leave me,' I said. 'I shall come back quickly.' I watched the rosy dawn outside the window. The hum of the breeze entered my head like an intoxicant. I saw the dark corridor shrinking from all four sides and finally surrounding me like a coffin made exactly to my size.

'Leave me,' I said a little loudly. 'I shall come back very soon. Don't stop me.'

Just then my husband pushed me with force. I felt strings snapping inside my mind and as I hurriedly searched for their ends, he pushed me again from behind. It was only by grasping the door of the bedroom that I could steady myself and stand up straight. Then I saw my husband's face just once, like the tip of a burnt out wick. Perhaps it is the expression I saw on his face that day that I call black fire. He wiped his oily hands on his chest and stomach and pushed me again onto the cot. As I fell, hitting my nose on the cot, my pride turning sour and fermented, I realised that yesterday, it was in such a moment that I had cried like a sub-human creature. I felt extremely frightened. My husband was about to close the door that led outside after bolting the windows of the bedroom.

Perhaps he would beat me. At least, after that I wanted to get out and walk for a while in the hot sun. Again, the image of fire, the flaming fire, came to my mind, an object of fascination. The fire that opens up and burns like a flower. Holding the door-latch my husband stood staring at me. On his shining neck the big ball rolled as he gulped the spit down. I wondered if he would continue to stare like that even when I rolled along the dark corridor. Then I realised that everything happening was real. The closed doors and the closed windows. I shrieked from the cot like a snake about to deliver: 'Let me out. I feel suffocated. I can't. . . .'

I thought I was suffocating. I was seized by an unbearable discomfort, hatred, anger and fatigue. In a trice I saw from where I stood the walls of my bedroom slowly being transformed into granite, and my husband melting away into nothingness, like water dripping from the pipe in the darkness that surrounded me. In that sorrowful loneliness, I ran to the door like a traveller who desperately jumps into the water from a sinking boat. My mind was filled with anger, despair and intense fear. 'Let me out.' I shouted: 'Otherwise, I will break this door open.'

In the engulfing silence my voice thickened as if coming from a disembodied being. I was alone in the silent darkness beyond the door that stood like a block before me, a terrible creature of the dark. I suddenly became silent with fear. I stared vacantly at that door. No, I think that what I said now is wrong. There wasn't any door. What I was anxiously looking at was the darkness. I felt like throwing myself at my husband's feet and begging him to show me the door and open it for me. Pride is a relative phenomenon. After all, I can not open any door with a mind weakened by fatigue. The pace of my own breath, like the hum of a wind passing by a dry, empty compound, provoked me into anger. At the back of my mind, I imagined an iron rod like the one that I had seen in my dream, plunging into my husband's neck, which to my mind seemed like a dried-up tree.

I walked round and round the room several times sniffing

at the four walls around me and growling like a wild beast, shut up in a cage. As the sound of my own breath and footsteps echoed in my ears like an all-encompassing roar my small room began to grow length-wise like a corridor. I started running to be able see the end of that narrow corridor with its bends and turns. As I ran fast in that utter darkness, I saw grains of light, as minute as the holes made by ants on the floor. Perhaps it was because I had nothing else to do other than to run that I ventured to scrape the plaster from the ceiling. Suddenly, the grains of light fell on me like sand. That was how I discovered the prince. The prince sat in full regalia, holding the sword, on a horse that stood with wings outstretched. From his laughter grains of light had fallen on my body.

The prince sitting on the glittering saddle stretched out his arms towards me, standing below. As I climbed, grasping his hand, and sat on his horse, the prince asked,

'What do you want?'

'I want to fly,' I said.

'Where to?' the prince asked.

I thought a great deal. Where shall I fly to? At last, I said, 'I don't know. Decide that yourself.'

The prince laughed, shedding grains of light. Then staring at the gem-studded locket which hung on his neck he said, 'Make her a princess.'

Suddenly I became a lovely princess adorned with various ornaments. The waves of the ocean were the pleats of the dress I wore. The gems I wore in my hair became stars.

'Now I will give the princess a sword,' he said. 'But if once you lunge with the sword, you cannot withdraw it without it having some effect.'

I went a long way with the prince holding that powerful sword, wearing that crown, and with a feeling of inexpressible self-confidence. Flying thus, I then saw my husband below, far below, at the door, like a watchman.

'Please leave me on the earth.' I told the prince. 'I shall return soon.'

I reached the earth very fast, like a bird's feather gliding down. There I stood before my husband with the sword, crown and all the decorations and an air of mighty haughtiness. For some minutes, he kept looking at me, now transformed into an extremely beautiful princess. Maybe because of the contemptuous smile that spread on my lips at his expression of disbelief and discontent, he pounced on me with the power and quickness of a hound. He struck off my golden crown in a split second. I have to admit that I had not expected this. We both tumbled together into the room like fighting dogs. By then my mind had become like a kite, with all the strings broken. Darkness gushed into it and foamed like a river in spate. In that darkness, as I saw the golden sword that had dropped from my hand lying among the myriads of objects scattered about, I felt humiliated like the princess beaten up by an enemy soldier. The prince might be seeing my defeat and humiliation from above. As I stared at the lean neck, devoid of masculinity, right before me, I remembered that I had to return immediately to the prince. Like a princess I pulled out the sword. I do not know whether it was his smooth neck that resembled the shining skin of a poisonous snake, or my unsheathed sword that prompted me to kill my husband. But all that is irrelevant. When he fell to one side, shocked, with his hands loosened, my husband's face was not as I expected it to be. Death makes all of us terribly worthless and foolish. The face of this man who had fallen and lay at my feet was incredibly like that of a clown. I covered my husband's body and head with a white dhoti that was hanging on the clothesline for drying. And as I did not feel tired, I tidied the crumpled sheet on our bed neatly and arranged the other scattered things. Come what may, there are some courtesies we should show towards death. Death comes to the prince and princess too. But I think I was late, in spite of the speed with which I did everything. The flying horse and the prince did not wait for me in the sky outside. The fault is mine. I should not have returned to the earth with the power of the sword. I must tell all this to the prince, that it is frightening for me to be alone and that I am throwing the sword away. But I have to wait. That is why I have begun to sit on these steps in front of the house. After all, it is my fault.

Translated by Jancy James
Published in Malayalam as : Raj Kumari ude Vaal

The Symphony of the Forest

SARAH JOSEPH

He heard his wife and children returning from their evening walk on the path outside. He stopped writing, got up, joined his hands behind his back and stretched to relieve his stiff limbs. Pressing his hands to his hips, he turned sideways, left and right. Then he added tea-leaves to the water boiling on the stove, and started the tea.

How many cups of tea she consumed in a day! Recently it had become excessive. She wouldn't listen to anything he said. Look at her, so thin and dried up, from drinking so much tea!

He poured milk into the kettle, and added sugar. Then he stored the decoction after draining out the leaves. She had mixed spices with the tea leaves. His nostrils flared as steam rose from the teapot. He liked fragrant tea. As for her, there was no other drink which she liked better.

The children came running into the room. He poured the tea into a cup, tasted it and moved to the front. She closed and bolted the gate and walked up the path, leading their young daughter by the hand. Her face was pale as paper. Even the big kumkum on her forehead seemed to have gone pale.

She darted a peculiar look at his face and stood below the steps, silent, her mind full of shadows. The vermilion powder on her forehead had begun to dissolve as drops of perspiration formed there.

'Yes?' He asked, raising his eyebrows. Her lips trembled like the petals of a flower, but she said nothing. Her curls rose and fell in the evening breeze. She raised her hand in a sudden movement and brushed back her hair. She bit her lip as though to stem the rising sorrow, and went inside.

He drank his tea in one gulp and followed her. 'The tea is getting cold,' he called out, looking inside.

'Biscuits, Give us biscuits. We want biscuits with the tea!' His sons came running, their school-bags hanging on their shoulders.

'Ask mother.'

She brought out cream biscuits and banana chips in a square plate. She looked down, perhaps to hide her tear-stained eyes. He poured the tea into the light brown tea-cups and held out a cup to her. She accepted it, taking special care to avoid his eyes. Her lips trembled once again. Keeping the tea on the table, she wiped her face with the edge of her sari.

'Why do you let the tea go cold? Why don't you drink it?' he scolded.

The children finished their tea, gathered their books and school-bags and ran to their room. They competed with each other in reading their lessons.

He went back to the bills and accounts spread out on the table. The youngest daughter had stayed back, eating her chips. She sat on the floor with her legs outstretched. The plate lay on her lap and she sang while she ate: 'The elephant is coming, the elephant with a trunk.' The little girl rocked back and forth. Every now and then, she glanced covertly at her mother and laughed.

The boys brought their progress cards to him to sign. He began to question them.

'Why can't you score a hundred marks in arithmetic?'

But it was evident from his tone that he was very proud of them for having scored more than eighty per cent in the subject. Still, he adopted an artificially stern tone and urged them to do better. Then, he looked covertly at her, signing with

from everything, intruded on her consciousness like the crescendo of a base drum.

'No, No, I don't want . . .

Panting hard, she ran inside.

'What is the matter?' Seeing her husband coming towards her she stopped abruptly. She opened her large eyes wide and stared at him, without flickering her eyelids. He looked away, disturbed. Like a gust of wind . . . .

Like a wind—she ran and fell into his arms.

'Please save me.'

'What?' He pushed her aside and looked around to see where the children were and asked in a harsh voice, 'Are you going mad? Save you? From what?'

'I . . .' She stopped halfway. And added inwardly . . . 'I was about to do something wrong.'

'You . . .' as he walked towards the bathroom, he said, 'you are going soft in the head.'

She stood still and stared at him, as he pushed her aside and walked away. Her outstretched hands, seeking protection, went down slowly.

In a trice, as though remembering something, she ran to her children. She held on to the door-frame, panting, and gazed at them unflinchingly. Rocking back and forth, her daughter had begun to doze off; parts of a small song, which had lost some words in the strands of sleep, lingered on her lips. She rushed in and picked her up. The child shuddered and awoke, stared at her mother intently for a few seconds and then leaned on her shoulder and slept.

'Won't you save me, darling?' She touched her cheek to the child's. Both were wet with tears.

She feared that she was the discordant note that stood apart from the symphony of the home. The feeling was unbearable to her.

Still, at night, when she lay awake, between him and the children, why did they not console her? She was angry. She got up and left them to stand near the window. She tried to invoke the symphony of the forest from the darkness outside. She coiled the imaginary lotus fibres around her eyelashes. She resurrected in her memory, the voice that reflected the joy of nature and filled her heart.

'Are you angry with me, Sati?'

'No, No, No, No.' Like a woman possessed, she gazed outside, shaking her head vehemently in negation.

Translated by Vasanthi Sankaranarayanan
Published in Malayalam as: Kadinte Sangeetam

Notes on Authors

LALITHAMBIKA ANTARJANAM (1909-87) is considered the mother of women writers in Malayalam. Although from a literary family in South Kerala, (both her parents wrote poetry), Lalithambika herself had little formal education and remained a political activist and social reformer all her life, being involved with the Indian National Congress and later with the Kerala Marxist Party. She has nine story collections, six poetry collections, two books for children and a novel to her credit. *Agnisakshi*, the novel, received the Kerala Sahitya Akademi award in 1980. Lalithambika's works are significant for their sympathetic portrayal of women of the Nambudiri community, who are oppressed by a crumbling, but powerful tradition.

SARA THOMAS: (b. 1934) a zoology graduate from Trivandrum, has published 15 novels and three short story collections. She is married to a doctor and has two daughters. For the novel *Narmadipudava* she received the Kerala Sahitya Akademi Award in 1974. Four of her novels have been filmed. She has been a member of the Kerala State Film Award Committee and is currently Member, General Council, Kerala Sahitya Akademi.

SHOBHA WARRIER: (date not known) a graduate in zoology, was educated in Kozhikode and Trivandrum. A freelance writer and columnist for several Malayalam and English dailies, she also writes radio plays. *Ramakundam* and *Meghana* are her notable story collections. Some of her stories have been translated into Telugu and Kannada. She is married and has a child.

B. SARASWATHY: (b. 1934), daughter of the famous short story writer Karoor Nilakantha Pillai, is a popular story writer in women's magazines. A retired teacher, some of her works appeared in major weeklies between 1952-65. *Karinja Pookal* (Faded Flowers) is a well-known story collection. She has also written two books of general prose.

K. SARASWATHI AMMA (1910-75) was the youngest daughter of a Nair family in Trivandrum. She worked as a teacher and then with the Kerala government as an accounts officer. A prolific writer, she published 12 volumes, containing over 100 short stories, and was the first self-proclaimed feminist in Malayalam literature. The last 15 years of her life were spent in mysterious silence, with not a single line penned; she died, unsung and neglected, in 1966. Among her published works are *Premabhajanam* (a novella); *Devadoothi* (a play); *Shreejanmam* (short stories); *Purushanmarillatha Lokam* (World Without Men, essays). Her first story was written in 1938. She disliked the institution of marriage and wilfully chose to remain single. Photography was an abiding hobby.

K.B. SREEDEVI (b. 1940) belongs to Malappuram district, north Kerala and was born of orthodox Nambudiri parents, steeped in Vedic learning. Finishing high school at just 13, she studied music. She also began writing stories. After her marriage to K.B. Namboodiripad three years later, she became a serious student of Sanskrit. Among her notable novels are *Yagnam*, *Chanakallu* (Touchstone), *Munnam Thalamurrai* (The Third Generation) and *Nirmala*, which was also made into a film and awarded the State Award for dialogue and story. *Kuttithirumeni* (The Young Nambudiri) and *Commonwealth* are her short story collections. Currently, she is researching the contribution of the ancient *gurukulas* to Kerala's cultural heritage.

M.D. RETNAMMA (b. 1944) is professor of Hindi in Sasthancotta, Quilon district. One of five children of Ponnakunnam Damodaran, a renowned Malayalam poet, she took her M.A. degree in Hindi from Kerala University and then became a lecturer in 1968. She has authored 18 novels and a collection of short stories in Malayalam entitled *Aparna*. A few of her stories have been translated into Kannada and Russian.

RAJALEKSHMY (1930-65) came from Ernakulam, where her father was a lawyer. An M.Sc. in Physics, she lectured at the

N.S.S. (Nair Service Society) college in Ottapalam, North Kerala and remained single. Her first story, a long piece *Makal* (Daughter) appeared in 1956. From a very young age, Rajalekshmy continued to be haunted by an unnameable fear, perhaps of death, all her life. Indeed, death appears as an important theme in her novels and stories, for example in her prose poem *Kumila* (Bubble) and the story *Atmahatya* (Suicide, 1964). Other works include a novel *Oru Vazhiyum Kure Nizhalukalum* (A Path and a Few Shadows). Her writings often reflected her perception of the inner lives of the people around her, which earned her their displeasure. It was perhaps this that drove her to suicide.

ASHITA (b. 1956), the second daughter of a naval officer, had her schooling in Delhi and Bombay and then obtained an M.A. in English from Kerala University. She now lives in Trivandrum where she writes on social issues, apart from being a creative writer. Ashita also writes poetry in English. *Othuthirppukal* (Compromises) and *Vismaya Chinhamgal* (Amazing Signs) are among her outstanding stories, the latter of which received the Edasseri Award.

KAMALA DAS (b. 1934), a well-known poet in English and an outstanding story writer in Malayalam, comes from an aristocratic Nair family with a literary tradition. Her mother, Balamani Amma, is considered the doyen among Malayalam poets and her late uncle, Nalapat Narayana Menon was a renowned litterateur. Notable among her 15 short story collections are *Thanuppu* (Coldness), *Tharisunilam* (Arid Land), *Chuvanna Pavada* (The Red Skirt), *Pakshiyude Manam* (The Smell of the Bird) and *Premathinte Vilapa Kavyam* (The Elegy of Love). Her collections of poems *Summer in Calcutta*, *The Descendants* and *The Old Playhouse* are well-known. Exploration of love and all its nuances, expressed in a strongly confessional tone, are typical of her writing. She has received several awards such as the Kumaran Asan Award and the Kerala Sahitya Akademi Award.

P. VATSALA (b. 1938), a high school teacher in Kozhikode, is known first for her novels and then her short stories. Responding strongly to contemporary social reality her writings reflect leftist leanings. Tribal life and the milieu of the Wynad (hilly forest regions) people are explored in depth in her novels, while her short stories focus on women's concerns. Acute concentration on the emotional aspect, and marginalization of the plot are characteristic of her stories. Her novels *Nellu* (Paddy), and *Nizhalurangunna Vazhikal* (Paths where the Shadows Sleep) received the Kumkumam Award and the Kerala Sahitya Akademi Award, with the former being made into a film.

P.R. SHYAMALA (1933-90) a popular writer, who featured often in Malayalam women's weeklies, came from a renowned Nair family of Trivandrum. At University she studied music and then moved to literature, having been inspired by her father's friend Takazhi Sivasankara Pillai. She has written 15 novels, three of which have been made into films and one, *Sararanthal*, (Chandeliers) into a successful television serial. Her works have been translated into Kannada, Gujarati and English.

NALINI BAKEL (b. 1955) comes of a Nair family of Bakel, Kasaragod district, on the border of Kerala and Karnataka. Though she could not complete her University degree, she won early recognition with her first novel *Thuruthu* (Promontory) which gained the first place in the novel-writing competition held by *Mathrubhumi* in 1977. She was co-editor of a women's weekly *Kumari*, for a short period. Her novels are *Hamsaganam, Krishna, Amma Daivangal* (Mother Goddesses) *Kanvathirtha* and *Ottakkolam*. Her collection of short stories *Muchilottama* has received the Edasseri Award. She is married to Payipra Radhakrishnan, a distinguished Malayalam writer, and has two children.

MANASI (b. 1948) once a prolific writer, has not written much recently. She projects a kind of interiority in her works in the portrayal of a woman's plight with a very strong current of feminism. *Idivaalinde Tengal* (Sob of Lightning) and *Manjilapakshi* (Bird in the Mist) are among her better known story collections.

SARAH JOSEPH (b. 1948) is professor of Malayalam in Palaghat and a political activist. Considered a radical with a pronounced feminist stance, she writes mostly about women struggling against the drudgery and ennui of domesticity. Lately, her stories have tended towards being 'fantasies of revenge'. As an activist, she formed the first feminist theatre group in Kerala and directed an anti-dowry play *Stri*. Her short story collections *Papathara* (Ground of Sin) *Kadinte Sangeetam* (Symphony of the Forest) and the novel *Nanma Thinmakalude Vriksham* (The Tree of Good and Evil) are among her highly acclaimed works.

GLOSSARY

Adaprathaman	A kind of thin milk pudding with *adas*, a kind of rice pasta
Asthithara	Appointed place in a Nair house, usually the courtyard for keeping the relics and the ashes of the departed
Avittam	The day after Onam
Bhagavatham	stories about Krishna
Chechi	Elder sister
Chingam	August and September, according to the Malayalam calendar
Dharmapatni	Dutiful wife
eight auspicious objects	Paddy, rice, sacred texts, saffron, sandal paste, collyrium, kumkum, newly washed cloth and ten sacred flowers. These were arranged in silver and bronze platters and used on every auspicious occasion
Magha	January and February according to the Malayalam calendar
Makaram	See Magha
Mandapam	Hall
Nalampalam	Corridor or pillared hall in a temple
Nalukettu	Traditional Nair house
Onappudava	A sari given at Onam
payasam	Thin milk pudding
Pradosham	A fast observed by women on the twelfth day of each half of the moon to get the blessing of Siva
pudava	gift of sari symbolising a relationship of matrimony
Sivabali	Offerings to Siva
Smartha	A woman accused of prostitution is tried by a court of Smarthas in the presence of a King. In Kerala it was the Nambudiris who were considered to be Smarthas

tali	A chain with a locket or a pendant which the bridegroom ties around the bride's neck during the marriage ceremony. Considered a symbol of faithfulness to the husband, the tali is removed only when the husband dies.
taravad	Matrilineal joint family in Kerala
Thampuran	A term of respect used for high caste Brahmins or Kshatriyas
Thampuratti	Wife of the Thampuran
tulasi	A string, usually worn by windows, made of the dried stem of the basil plant
Vadakkini	The northern side of a Nalukettu
Vaidyan	A practitioner of indigenous medicine
Vaishakha	May and June according to the Malayalam calendar
Valkalam	Drape of bark generally worn by mendicants
Varam	Recital of verses from the Vedas by Nambudiri's in temples, usually followed by a feast